LOVE
POWER
POLITICS!!

Books by the same author

Love, Life & a Beer can!

If I Pretend I am Sorry!

It wasn't Love at First

LOVE
POWER
POLITICS!!

Prashant Sharma

Srishti
PUBLISHERS & DISTRIBUTORS

Srishti Publishers & Distributors
N-16, C. R. Park
New Delhi 110 019
srishtipublishers@gmail.com

First published by
Srishti Publishers & Distributors in 2013

All characters in this book are fictitous, and any resemblance to real persons, living or dead, is coincidental.

Typeset by EGP at Srishti

Suchi and Prabhat

And a lifetime of Happiness!

PROLOGUE

I was running frantically and I could see a sea of police behind me.

My short hair, all gelled, in stark comparison to the way they were when I had been running with Hari on the same lanes three years ago. I was dressed in a kurta-pyjama, Radha had told me that it would help me go unnoticed in the crowd. My attention then shifted towards Radha. Was she fine or had she also been caught by the police?

I suddenly did not know why I was running, and suddenly unsure if someone was even following me, but I was running. I looked back and they were there. I was leading them by a good distance, but I knew it was just a matter of time, just a matter of time before they got to me, the way the Gandhi Bhavan seniors had got to Hari and me three years ago.

Just then a stone was thrown at me which just passed my head. I did not look back. I kept on running. I could not make the same mistake my dear friend Hari had made. I got into the market, running over stalls, jumping around some people and crashing into some others. The market was as crowded as you would expect in a small town in Rajasthan with the narrowest of by lanes and a chief minister in town to hoist the Independence day flag in our University. A scooter was in front of me- it was a déjà vu moment. I think I had lived the moment before, but with someone else.

I knew what to do. I ran towards the scooter, and I pulled the man down. The plan was not as effective with only one person instead of two but the man fell down nevertheless. The scooter now occupied the by lane in entirety and the little man was under it. It helped me get a little ahead of the pack that was following me.

I ran more. I ran faster.

Just when I thought I had lost them, one of the chasers, in a last ditch attempt, picked up another stone and threw it at me. This time I made the mistake of looking back. On an impulse, I moved to the right and caught a person on a cycle, both of us landing with a thud on the ground.

I knew it was over then. The police came and hit me on my head with a gun and carried me towards the waiting jeep. The plan which we, Radha and I, had made was fool proof but somehow we had been caught. I wondered what had happened to Radha. Had she also been caught? If not, then I would not give her away. She was like my little sister.

Just then I saw her. She was looking at me from a distance. But still, over all that distance, I could make out what had happened. I was pushed into the jeep and was taken away.

10 YEARS LATER

I was with ten other men. Each headed in the same direction. All of them had a reason, or at least it seemed as if they had a reason. I just followed them.

We were in a cave, or maybe a dungeon. I did not remember much of it. And we were running. I did not know whether we were chasing or being chased. But we were running. Crawling, swimming, wading our way past whatever came through, but nevertheless, running.

And then there were the sun rays. I think I had seen the sun after months, or maybe it was minutes. But the rays hit my eyes hard and the sudden burst of light made my eyes go blind and took me back to a better world. A world where I loved, a world where I was loved, a world which had meant something, a world which had now ceased to exist, a world which I was not even sure had existed.

I woke up startled. I had seen the same dream all over again. There was this constant urge in the dream to run away from the jail, to finish some unfinished business. But I could never make out what.

I did not remember much of what had happened in prison over the years. At times when I did get back my senses, I could hear other members of the jail taunting me that I was mad.

I was in one of my saner modes today and I went to the common area in the jail. I picked up the newspaper and read the headline.

"Radha Malik elected as the first lady MP"

Slowly it all came back to me.

*Love
Power
Politics!!*

GOPAL'S STORY

I was running frantically and Hari was running with me. My wavy hair all pulled back, in stark comparison to the bald head Hari was carrying around. We were dressed to deceive but in those days, I was very particular about my hair and hence did not do anything that would affect the style. The people who had sent me had earlier asked me to get my hair into shape- the way Hari had, because it always helped you get away unnoticed. All people on my side of the fence had near bald heads, but there were not many things in this world which I liked more than my hair.

A stone was thrown at us which just passed my beloved hair. I did not look back. I kept on running. We got into the market, running over stalls, jumping around some people and crashing into some others. The market was as crowded as you would expect in a small town in Rajasthan with the narrowest of by lanes. A scooter was in front of us and I looked at Hari and he looked at me. I think that was the moment when the bond was formed. We both knew what to do. We ran towards the scooter, either one on one side and we pulled the man down. The scooter now occupied the by lane in entirety and the little man was under it. It helped us get a little ahead of the pack that was following us.

We ran more. We ran faster.

Just when we thought we had lost them, one of our chasers, in a last ditch attempt, picked up another stone and threw it at us. I did not take the liberty to look back but Hari, in a moment of stupor, had made the mistake and he saw the piece of stone headed right towards him. On an impulse he moved to his right and caught a person on a cycle, both of them landing with a thud on the ground.

Our motorbike was parked right around the corner and we had to get to it and out of the area before our faces could be seen. I could have left Hari right there in the mess and could have ridden to safety. But the moment we had, the moment when our eyes had met and when we had both known what had to be done, I knew that life was too short and there were too little such moments and people in life to let go of. So I also stopped. Stopped and went back to pick up Hari but I knew I had been too late. I knew this was over. We had been caught, caught by the rival hostel gang.

So this is me, Gopal. I am eighteen years old. Tall, lanky, a failure of the academic system that has been built by our country, but nevertheless an engineer. Okay, not an engineer yet, but an engineering college student. More importantly-a first year engineering college student.

My parents had the same dream six lakh parents have every year. That their son would become an engineer. They did not dream IITs, in fact, I don't even think they knew what IIT was. They just thought that if I became an engineer I would somehow lead a better life than what I would have if I stayed back in the village and took over my father's shop. I, on the other hand, was not too sure about it. I tried to stay away from studies as much as possible and I knew that whatever was done to make me study, could not work out in my favour.

So like so many other parents, my father took a loan and sent me to Kota for preparation. He had a small shop where he used to sell daily supplies. We are a Brahmin family and a saying goes in the part of Rajasthan we are from, that a Brahmin cannot do business. I think the saying was based on my father. His friends, my friends, my mother's friends, our neighbours, our relatives (which was a huge number in itself), our enemies, people who knew, people who we did not know, so basically, practically anyone in the village was welcome to have tea at my father's shop. Being a gracious host, my father never said no, and in fact, would open a packet of biscuits from the shop. Obviously, it was all on the house. People could take anything they wanted and could pay as they pleased. And as it happened, not pay at all.

The only person my father could say no to, was me.

"Father, may I go and play outside?"

"No."

"Father, can you give me ten rupees?"

"No."

"Father, can I be a film star when I grow up?"

"No."

"Father, can I have some of what you are drinking?"

"No."

"Father, can I go to the toilet?"

"No. I mean what?"

"Father, can I go to the toilet?"

"Son, have I ever said no to you for that?"

Well honestly, he had once. He was scolding me for not doing well in my exams, which was an annual occurrence by the way. You think he would get used to it, but no.

So he was scolding me once and right when his anger went out of control and he raised his hand to slap me, I stopped him mid way and asked if I could go to the toilet then.

And yes, he said no.

I used to be a fun child when small. Happy, always smiling,

always playing, always finding new ways to irritate my father. But as I grew up, some sort of anger started to grow within me. And my father thought that making me study was the way to keep me in tabs.

So he decided that I would be an engineer. Some far flung son of his far flung cousin had managed to become an engineer in some far flung college and that is the reason my father wanted me to become one. Not that that far flung son was doing anything in life, he was also running a shop a stone's throw away, but he used to tell stories about what his other batch mates did, and one day he would too. That excited my father no end.

I obviously had no say in my future. And honestly I did not even care because *wanting* to be an engineer in our town meant going to Kota for IIT coaching. Neither my father, nor I, and I bet no one in the village knew where the IITs were, but as the system of our country goes, my father wanted to send me to prepare for the exam.

If you were in Rajasthan and were preparing to be an engineer, you just had to go to Kota. It was as important as the engineering degree itself. So I left for Kota. Leaving behind my mother, my father, my whole village and carrying with me a dream. A dream which my father had dreamt for me.

So I lived in Kota. For three years of my life. My father took a loan every year but I bet the way others did not pay his loan, he did not pay his either.

But he was a good man. He cared for me. The way he showed the care was a little unconventional.

So I was in Kota. The only phase of my life which I regret and I have done lots of things worth regretting. Not because I did not make it to any good engineering college, that was a given with my level of sincerity for studies, but because in those three years I could not get to make any people my own. I always believed, that when needed, it would be the people who would stand by you, not the degrees.

Only to be wronged later.

The three years there were actually a hell hole which ended with me getting admitted to some college in some far flung area of the state. My parents were happy, I was going to become an engineer even though I had flunked class twelve once (hence the three years instead of two in Kota). And I honestly could not care less where I was going as long as I was getting out of the dreaded Kota.

My college was not the type of college you read about in books or see in Shah Rukh Khan movies. It was a part of a huge University and the University was a place where people had only learnt one thing- power is above all. The University was divided into 3 major groups- on the basis of caste - as most things in the smaller parts of our country are, and there was always the constant struggle as to which group would become the President of the University. The President would then gradually enter the local politics of the area, and in fact, the current MLA of the region used to be the University President and was from my caste and my hostel.

This was the dream which every small town boy who entered the University saw. These were the young boys who had practically lived as slaves their entire life and the dream was that by winning power in college, they would one day be transformed from a nobody in the society- to a king.

So when we entered the college, we were given hostels on the basis of our castes. I, being a Brahmin, got the hostel where all the Brahmins stayed which was ironically called the Ambedkar Bhavan. The ragging in the campus was also not the ragging you hear or talk about. We were pretty much treated as slaves by the seniors and had to do all sorts of things for them. They would abuse us- get really bad with the words, hit us, torture us, all in the name of making Ambedkar Bhavan better than the Gandhi Bhavan and the Nehru Bhavan. I don't know how caning every day would help in making our BBhavan better, but apparently it did.

So the ragging episodes lasted for about a month where we were basically treated like shit and were tossed around from one senior to the other. Then came the part where we had to prove our supremacy over the other hostels.

The hostel rivalry was what legends are made off. Ours was a fairly old University, dominated earlier by the courses in arts. At that time, Nehru Bhavan was the one which controlled all power and all decisions of the University. But gradually, as other courses started, the other two Bhavans started gaining in prominence and as the current day stood, with the maximum number of students in engineering, Gandhi and Ambedkar Bhavan used to fight it out.

There used to be stories of power and dominance, no one knew how true, which were passed from generation to generation of students and by the time the ragging period ended, it was etched in our minds that the only reason we existed, was to sacrifice ourselves for the sake of our Bhavan.

After a host of ragging activities, we were now down to the last stage. This stage involved tasks to be performed on alien territory.

So Hari and I were selected for the first task. Our task was simple. The leader of Gandhi Bhavan had a thing for a girl in the second year. And as you would imagine, the situation of girls, handful that they were, was not much better than the fresher's.

So, the leader of Gandhi Bhavan, Surya, had a thing for a girl in the second year. Our task was simple. We had to paint an obscene picture of a girl, click a photo of the girl the senior liked, and super impose her face on the picture. The girl in the meanwhile, was oblivious of the fact that the life or maybe even death of two first year students depended on this. She in fact was even oblivious of the fact that the Gandhi Bhavan senior was in love with her. Obviously there was the eve teasing, but for her, and all other girls in the area, that was more of a norm than an aberration. She would have been surprised though that the eve teasing had stopped completely from one section of the college- the Gandhi Bhavan hostellers. In fact, they even bashed up quite a few people for her.

And she continued to live in oblivion that more than twenty bottles had been smashed on twenty heads because of her.

So Hari and I- both of zero morals, drew an insanely obscene picture of a girl. Anyways, morals come into the picture when you live. And in order to live, we had to do this. So we drew an insanely obscene picture of the girl. We took hold of a camera of one of the richer first year students and I was given the duty of clicking the picture and I obviously had to be very secretive about it.

I hung around a pan shop, which mainly catered to the Ambedkar Bhavan and was ready with the camera. But then she came in front of me, and I was too mesmerized to move.

To say she was beautiful would be the biggest understatement. She was fair, had a dimpled chin and a dimple on the right side of her cheek. Her nose was small and pointed, her cheeks looked soft and supple, just like a baby would have them, she had the deepest eyes which held back way more than what they gave away, her hair were shoulder height and were tied neatly behind, she would be five feet two, a little on the plump side with an angelic glow. She was dressed in Indian salwaar kameez with her dupatta tied behind her back.

She passed me and I had the camera in my hand. But I did not move. My eyes moved with her, trying to get hold of her eyes, but they did not meet and she passed by.

I moved out of the Pan shop and shouted, "Madam, have a look at our side as well."

I may be mesmerised but I was not the best with the words.

The whole world turned around and looked at me. Ours was a town where you gawked at girls, talked bad things about girls, drew dirty pictures of girls, you teased girls but you never, you never talked to girls. And that too senior girls. They were to be as distant to you as power was distant to our current prime minister.

But I did not know all that. And even if I did, I did not care. So I repeated "Madam. I said hello." With a greater stress on the 'd' and the second 'm' of madam, not to forget the street smart smile on my face which when coupled with my long hair and lean body, would have definitely made me look, well you know what it would have made me look.

The whole world had already turned around, but after I spoke for the second time, even she looked back. And our eyes met. For the first time.

A couple of seniors of my hostel quickly realised what this could lead to and I was whisked away by them quickly but never did I let go of her eyes, and she of mine. Her friends took her away and as I was being taken away I could hear their silent whispers and I think I even heard a laugh.

But work was after all work. I tried a couple of more times to take her picture but the same procedure repeated itself. I started off with the 'Madam' and stress on the 'd' and the 'm' and our eyes would meet and we would both be whisked away.

Hari finally took her picture. I asked him to take two and I kept one in my wallet, as a symbol of my love.

So we pasted one of the photos on the obscene picture and we were ready with our task. We had to paste the picture on the notice board of the Gandhi Bhavan at 1 pm in broad daylight.

Hari and I set out. We had barely met a couple of days back when it was decided that the two of us would do this particular task. We took a senior's motorcycle and parked it at a safe distance from the Gandhi Bhavan. The rule in Gandhi Bhavan was that all freshers in Gandhi Bhavan had to be seen in the hostel in only a vest with no shirt on. So we also removed our shirts and entered. There were too many new students for anyone to realise who is from which hostel. We were carrying the paper with us. 1 pm was when the mess started serving food and there were lots of people around. The notice board was close to the mess entrance. One senior accosted us "Who are you? What are you two doing here? Don't you know that the mess time for the freshers starts after the seniors are done with their food?"

We honestly did not know that. In our hostel, freshers were not allowed food in the mess for the first two months. Hari looked at me. He had a lump in his throat already. His eyes were just about to water when I replied "Sir, Rajesh sir told us to cover the notice board with cloth as otherwise the dust will spoil it. We told him that it was the senior's lunch time but he said that it was an order and had to be done now. Sorry sir."

The senior looked at us and smiled. He was among the more lenient ones. He slapped Hari on the back of his head and left. A tight slap mind you, not a playful one. Hitting us seemed their birthright. Each hostel was as bad as the other.

I opened the bag which we were carrying. We had cloth of the size of the notice board with us. I had planned this very meticulously. The drawing of the girl was in my pocket We stuck the picture to the notice board and quickly covered it with the cloth. As we were now working, none of the other seniors paid much attention to us.

Our work was slowly done. The board was covered with cloth and behind the cloth was the drawing. A day before I had torn the cloth from the center into two pieces and had then stitched it together. I had left one end of the stitch open and had left around 20 metres of thread lying lose.

We looked at the notice board which was now covered with the cloth with the picture behind it. I started leaving and took

Hari along with me. Hari was confused as to what I was doing. The task was to put the drawing on the board so that it would be visible to all. Not hide it behind some piece of cloth. But then, Hari was never a leader. He was a follower and would always be one. I held the lose piece of thread and we both started moving. After the twenty metres, the thread became taut and the cloth slowly started ripping from the middle.

And we started running.

Slowly the whole cloth was ripped off and the photo lay in full display for everyone to see.

We already had a head start of 50 metres by the time anyone realised what had happened and I trusted my legs to make peace with that.

It was a brilliant plan but for the stone which Hari tried to evade and ultimately had us caught.

As we ran in the by lanes of the town, Hari had tried to evade the stone and as with many other things in life, he was unsuccessful. He not only took the man on the cycle with him down but the stone also hit him on his head. He lay there, blood gushing out of a small wound in his big empty head. I was 20 metres in front of him, the motorbike which would take me to safety was right in front of me and a guy I had barely known for two days was lying in a pool of blood. I had to make my choice, and I chose him. The hosteller in me had finally taken over. I was not going to let the Gandhi Bhavan dictate to the Ambedkar Bhavan. Not that my presence would have made any difference, but that is what hostel life is all about. Crazy stupid unity, which would ultimately lead to everyone's downfall.

The students running after us had lost all hope of catching me. They had one guy and that was enough. They would make an example of him and teach the freshers of our hostel to stay away. The freshers of both hostels had been given tasks to do with the enemy hostel and we were the first ones caught.

Around 10 of them were surrounding Hari, kicking him, teasing him, playing with him. Hari was dead terrified. He was a small town boy, who had actually gone to Kota to study and make it through to a good engineering college. He was very hard working but not that smart. In fact, he was pretty dumb. He was the kind who would sit on the first bench, study the whole day, but still not do well. And he was shit scared. In the last two days we had spent together, he told me that he had thought of going back to his village every day. But he was too scared to think what other people would say to him. He had a kind of a demi God status in his village. He was the first person in the village who was becoming an engineer, irrespective of which college. He was so scared and under confident, that he could not even give up.

So they were circling Hari and were scaring him even more.

"We should make an example of him so that the bloody Ambedkar Bhavan knows where its place is. In shit."

"Let's show them what kind of ragging we do at Gandhi Bhavan. We will get him ragged by our freshers."

A fresher getting ragged by another fresher was the biggest insult that a person could take in our college.

"We will keep him in the dark room of our hostel and will not let him go out of the hostel for 2 days with no water or food."

"We will bloody strip him naked and leave him in the girl's hostel."

All of them were making these tall claims to scare the living hell out of Hari and having a good laugh about it. And they were doing a pretty good job. Hari by now had forgotten that he had a bleeding head and was crying profusely on hearing what was being said. The tears flowing from his eyes acted as fodder for the seniors and they continued abusing and scaring him.

I, meanwhile, was outside this hallowed circle so far. They had not even tried to catch me after getting Hari. And I knew that they would try and scare me the same way, and I would definitely get a big beating if they got hold of me.

I weighed my options once more, the bike ride to safety, or surrendering to save a stranger. I don't know why, but I chose the latter.

I knew they would hit me, but I was sure they could not scare me. And I thought I would take at least one or two of them down with me.

I approached the group and I charged towards one of them but the person in front of him saw me and before I knew what happened, he picked me and threw me on Hari. I was pretty strong myself, living in a village in Rajasthan and doing all sorts of manual labor as a kid had made me lean but very fit and strong, but I did not know what had hit me. The person who took charge of me would have been at least ten times stronger.

Hari and I were both lying in a heap on the ground, Hari bleeding from his head and me from my elbows. The light hearted bantering had now changed to a more serious tone. They were baffled by my audacity. They were surprised that someone could be so stupid to pick up a fight with ten seniors of a rival hostel and that to in their own den!

We were lifted and were dragged to the Gandhi Bhavan. The bike which I had brought was now ridden by one of them and we were *placed* in the centre courtyard of the Gandhi Bhavan, a place where everyone could see the treatment that was reserved for us. Our bike was parked right next to us. And just then Surya walked out, the Gandhi Bhavan leader.

So these two are the mother fuckers who dared spoil the image of my Radha."

Her name was Radha. The name of my love was Radha. I suppressed a smile. An ass licker added to it. "Surya, the one with the long hair also tried to put up a fight."

Surya was standing at a distance of ten feet from us. He raised his hand towards the ass licker who quickly shut up. Slowly a crowd was gathering around us. He barked again, "Ravi, get me the photo they have painted."

Ravi obeyed and Surya saw the picture again and this time he could not control his anger and he kicked me in my gut. I silently thanked God that he kicked me and not Hari. Ambedkar Bhavan's reputation was on line here.

He grabbed me by my hair. As I had mentioned my hair were very dear to me. They were shoulder length and I had managed to save them from the seniors in my hostel even though all other freshers were made to go bald. I had told them that I had been growing them for religious reasons and once you got religion in between in these areas of Rajasthan, no one doubted your motive. So I was allowed to have the long flowing tresses. But not for long.

Someone in the meanwhile had got a razor and Surya used the razor on my head taking away a good chunk of my hair. If I would have ever cried in my life, that moment would have been it. But I let it pass.

"Take them to the dungeon." With this, we were handed our sentence and Surya left. And then he came back, a matchstick in his hand, and he opened the petrol tank, lit the matchstick and put it in.

That day, as I, along with a lot many people, was running away from the burning bike, I realised what power meant in these circles. I realised what politics meant to a student community. And I realised what student politics was. It was not about the President seat. It was about power. Raw power.

We did not get to run very far, Hari and I. The order of Surya had to be executed. We were to be sent to the *dungeon*. I did not know what scared Hari more, the dungeon or the beating we would get when we went back to our own hostel and would have to tell our seniors that they had burnt the bike. Hari was petrified. He was in the situation where he had ceased to react. He wore a blank look on his face, the blood still oozing from his head, and tears rolling down his cheeks. I had never seen a man so helpless. I did not want to be seen like that in front of anyone so I took control over myself and tried to build a confident and aloof countenance. I looked up, into their eyes instead of looking down. I would not go down crying.

I got one tight slap on my cheek and this time it was the absolute insult. I had been slapped by a fresher. Everyone was laughing at me all of a sudden. My head went down, partly in shame and embarrassment, and partly in fear.

We were escorted to the dungeon. Hari had been in the same state of shock all this while with the blank face and the tears rolling down his cheeks. I on the other hand was wondering what this dungeon was. On the way from the foyer to the dungeon, the people who were escorting us had tried to scare the hell out of us by telling us all weird stories which ranged from the plausible- that it is infested by rats, to the possible that we will get no food, to the improbable that a spirit lives there. But whatever done and said, they had managed to scare the crap out of Hari.

So we finally reached the dungeon. It was basically the crap area of the fourth floor toilet. We both were pushed inside and the door was shut behind us. Our eyes slowly got better of the dark, and we could see each other's silhouette. Hari was still in the same mode. I looked around and saw a toilet which I don't think was in a usable condition. There were no windows, and in fact there seemed nothing else but the non usable lavatory. I did not know how long we were to be kept in this. I just hoped it was not too long. We were not *real* prisoners. After all, the only thing we did was that we posted an obscene picture of the girl which the hostel leader, and now even I, loved.

I spoke to Hari to enquire how he was doing but he seemed in a different world altogether, so I put my head down on a rock, and I slept.

After I don't know how much time, I was woken by Hari. My eyes again took some time getting used to the pitch dark but then I saw Hari staring at me.

"Why did you come back?"

"Come back where?"

"Come back to save me?"

"We are stuck in this shit hole of a room, and that is all you ask of me? Why did I come to save you? Why the fuck did you fall down? Why the fuck did you look back? How the fuck do we get out of here?"

"Why did you come back?"

I gave a long pause. I knew he demanded an answer. An answer which I did not know.

"I don't know why I came back. I guess we were in this together."

"No one has done such a thing for me. Ever."

Another tear rolled down his cheek. For a guy, he cried way too much. And then he spoke again.

"Thanks. I will never forget this. If you ever need me, just let me know. I have never said this to anyone but I will do anything you want of me. Anything."

More tears and a long pause later, I spoke.

"Now stop the crying you little baby. You got us in here. Now you have to get us out."

A faint smile appeared on his face. A very welcome change from the face which he had been showing me for a hell lot of time.

"Why the hell are you smiling. Am I cracking some fucking joke here?"

He smiled some more. It actually felt nice to see someone smile.

"Why the fuck are you smiling?"

"I had once read, that if you are put in jail, your good friend will bail you out, but your real friend would be sitting right next to you and blaming you for getting both of you caught."

He then smiled some more, and then started laughing.

I did not really know how to react, so I also started laughing. Suddenly the door opened and the people who had come to check on us saw us laughing our hearts out.

"You mother fuckers think this is funny, now you will be here for another twenty four hours."

We both looked at them, and we both continued our laughing. We knew that we had made friends forever. But then, as someone has said- *forever is a very long time.*

The laughing, though it seemed pretty funny at the moment, gave us twenty four more hours inside that dreaded hell hole. We talked a lot when we were inside, mainly because there was nothing else really we could do. We talked and we slept. Hari told me on his inner most feelings, how he knew that he was under confident and very scared of rejection and how he hated the college we were in and how he deserved something much better and how every moment he spent here, he wanted to run away. Run away back to the village where he came from. Run away to peace, run away to a place where you did not have to make obscene pictures of girls, run away to a place where you were not put in a 3 by 3 hell hole.

"It's strange isn't it. We think that the answers to our happiness lie in a degree, or in a job, or in some money. But deep within, we all know what we really want. I want to live the life my father leads. I want to go back to my village, work on the fields and earn just enough to feed me and my family. You know something, he is the happiest man I have ever seen. Maybe because he does not want anything more than what he has. The only wish of his that was unfulfilled was that his son studies and gets a degree. And that is the reason I have not run away yet. I want to fulfil his dream. I know I can never be good at what we study, maybe because I am not that smart, or maybe because I just don't want to be.

But leave all that, I can go on and on ranting about the perfect life in the village. You tell me, why are you here and what do you want?"

That day I realised something about Hari. I don't know how or what made me think so, but I came to know that he had a very smart and intelligent mind. And this would be something that would be proved to me over and over again in the coming years.

I then told him my story.

"Honestly, I don't know why I am here. I guess same reason as you. Parents wanted me to do this, and at that time, I was too young to rebel. But now I know what I want. I want to be the President of this University. And you wait and watch, I will be the President of this University. I will play all my cards right."

"Haha, and I will be the President's friend."

"Yes, you will be the President's friend."

We kept on chatting and gradually Hari dozed off. I thought about what he had just said. He was not as stupid or dumb as I had initially thought he was. He knew that he wasn't the smartest, and the fact that he knew this, covered up for it. I remembered the excitement on his face when he had said that he would be the President's friend. And then I realised that how all of a sudden that had come out of my mouth. Did I really want to be the President?

I think I did.

Dreaming about how grand life would be and what I would do after I became the President, I also dozed off.

We were awakened by the same senior who had come the day before and had heard us laughing and had granted us one more day inside the hell hole which they called the dungeon. He kicked me and Hari and asked us if we again thought the whole thing was very funny.

I was about to retort but before I could say anything Hari realised that my words would lead to one more day inside so he started howling. This time the senior from the Gandhi Bhavan laughed and he allowed us out.

The sending off was not as grand as in swearing in. We were both kicked a couple of times but this time there was no coterie of 10 people surrounding us. Just the lone senior who lead us out of the Gandhi Bhavan hostel gate.

We both made the long walk back to the hostel. We had both not bathed, had not eaten anything for quite some time. In fact, we did not even know how long we had been in there and what day and time it was. I, in particular, was looking very hideous with a bald patch in between my otherwise long flowing tresses. I asked one kid who was walking around the road what time and day it was and he ran away saying 'ghost' 'ghost'.

He did overdo it a tad bit, but he wasn't that way off. That helped me and Hari have another laugh before we entered our hostel and received a similar treatment from our seniors. We continued our walk towards Ambedkar Bhavan, not sure of what would happen, and not caring about what day it was because honestly, it just did not matter. We had failed in the task assigned to us, though I sincerely hoped we got marks for trying and for ingenuity, we had sacrificed a motorbike belonging to one of the seniors of our hostel, we had been humiliated, and had hence humiliated Ambedkar Bhavan in front of Gandhi Bhavan. We were guilty, and were prepared to face another round of punishment. Well, at least I was. The same detached look came on Hari's face again. I think he was ready as well.

We entered the hostel gates and were greeted by the worker in our mess who could not control a smile when he saw me. We quietly retired into our rooms.

I finally looked into a mirror and was horrified on what I saw. The bastard had shaved of my head right from the centre and I was really looking like a ghost. Devoid of all emotion, I took out a razor and shaved the remaining part of my head. Had I been Hari, I would have been crying like a baby on doing that. I hated Gandhi Bhavan and their leader Surya. He was going to stand for elections and I made a promise to myself that I would not let him win.

I would do whatever it took to defeat him.

There was a loud bang on my door. Rakesh, a senior from the second year was there. Hari was already with him. We were going to be tried again, and this time in our own court. He asked me to follow him and I did. Hari was again looking as scared as he had been in the enemy hostel.

Prithvi, the leader of our hostel was standing in the foyer and all the freshers were already there. His lashings had been reserved for special occasions when an example had to be set for the other freshers that this is what is going to happen if you misbehave.

We were asked to stand right behind him. He turned back, he moved towards us. Both of us closed our eyes and tightened our cheeks. We dare not put our hand on them or try to avert the slap, the consequences would have been grave. But instead of slapping us, he hugged us, first Hari and then me. He then faced the hostel and spoke.

Prithvi-"This is the reason we rag you. To make you tough. To make you worthy of being called a member of the Ambedkar Bhavan. I have heard that when after ten hours of confinement, the door was opened to these two young boys here, instead of pleading for mercy, they were laughing. Laughing at that mother fucker Surya and his hostel. I am proud of you my boys."

He raised his hands, and as you would expect in a movie, there was applause all around.

"Tell me, what have you learned out of all this?"

Hari spoke first- "I learnt that I belong here."

More applause. He basked in its glory. The scorn on his face turned into a full blown smile. Now it was my turn.

"I have learned to not forgive. Surya will pay for what he has done. Prithvi sir, I promise to you that you will be the next President of this University. I promise."

This was greeted with more applause and this time even Prithvi joined in. He came and hugged me again.

"This is the attitude I want in each and every one of you hostellers. I want each and every one of you to be as brave and as fearless as these two boys have shown us."

Slowly, the whole crowd dissipated and Hari and I were invited to have lunch with Prithvi. It was considered a very very big honor.

We talked about general college during lunch and Prithvi told me that even they had a dungeon sort of place in our hostel which was currently occupied by two freshers of Gandhi Bhavan. But unlike us, they had wailed their hearts out. Hari took a long sip of water, luckily the stories of his wailing had not reached Prithvi. I just smiled in pride.

The conversation veered from us and Prithvi started talking to other seniors. There was some talk about the current MLA of the region, a former President and part of Ambedkar Bhavan, and how he had promised 5 lac rupees to our hostel party. Prithvi was the President candidate but from the look of it, and from the general chit chat, I could make out that Surya had a very good chance this time. Apparently, the ratio of freshers from his caste to our caste was greatly skewed in his favour. And fuck democracy, and statesmanship, casteism was the way to garner votes. And the freshers' votes would make the difference.

The other seniors blamed the administration and even went to the level that Surya and his party had given money to the administration to skew the ratio. But Prithvi knew better. He knew that he could not undo what had already been done, and if Surya had actually bribed the administration in admitting more students from his caste, it was a very smart move from his side. He had started thinking of the elections way before our party had.

We were mere spectators to this discussion. What I had said regarding not letting Surya be the President was treated at face value, was treated as the hot blood of vengeance speaking which would cool down in a day or two. But no one in that room that day knew that I would be the one who would make all the difference in these elections.

Another month passed and we, the freshers, gradually settled into the college life. We had to do some assignments of the seniors but that is what ragging was now limited to. My hair were also growing back, though they would take their own sweet time in becoming the mane which they were earlier.

We settled into the regular monotony of a third grade engineering college where the teachers did not care, and the students cared even less. The only exciting thing that was happening was the elections, and of course, Radha.

So Radha and I had hooked up. Yes, we were kind of seeing each other and she being the crush of Surya, we obviously had to keep our relationship in the wraps. Anyways, the type of place we were in, it was not ideal to walk hand in hand. She was after all a senior. Had anyone come to know about us, I would have been thrashed to near death and even my hostel would not have done anything to save me. I had done practically nothing after my initial heroics. Even the assignments which I did for my seniors were not up to the mark.

The only person who knew about us besides Radha and I was Hari.

It had started in very casual manner. After I had shaved of my hair due to what Surya had done to them, I continued life in the same vein. But around a week later, Radha passed by, and smiled. It was the faintest smile you would ever see, and if I had not been in absolute love with her, I would have missed it too. But I knew what that smile meant. You just know when you know.

It was not a ridiculing smile, it was a smile of wonder. It was a smile which asked more questions than it gave answers, just like her eyes did. It was a smile which only someone in love can give.

She later told me that she knew that half of the college loved her, and the other half lusted her, but no one had ever dared talk to her the way I had. They had teased her, chased her, but never did they have the courage to say anything directly to her. She was the daughter of the biggest landlord in the city and had anyone crossed the line with her, that person would have been history.

I obviously had not known that, when I had talked to her for the first time. But when I approached her for the second time, I was fully aware of who and what she was.

I approached her after a week of the sly smiles. She had completely taken over me. She was all I could think about, all I could dream about. In fact she was all I *wanted* to think or dream about. I was a little hesitant to talk to her, because of the whole lineage and Surya, but the next time I saw her, I gave her a big smile, showing all my teeth. She looked down, showed me all her teeth, and ran away blushing.

And the next time, I approached her.

"You smile like an angel" and as an after thought "Madam." Again stressing on the M and the D. I had a big smile on my face. The smile typical of an eve teaser. But she saw more than that in it.

She whisked me aside and quietly asked me to meet her in the garden behind her house at night.

I did as I was told.

I took a seniors bike and left to meet Radha in the richer part of the town. I had limited knowledge about her and her family but I knew that her father was amongst the richest men in the area. I reached her haveli and was pretty impressed by its size. There were guards positioned at the front gate and I moved around trying to get a glimpse of how to break in. She had asked me to meet her at the park behind her house at 10. In anticipation and excitement, I had reached there at 9. I made a couple of more rounds, upped the concern of the guards a little and went behind the haveli.

It was a nice little park. I assumed it would be full of children and their mothers in the morning but right now there were some drug addicts and some swamis living in their own world. I could see Radha's room in front of me. It was on the first floor, was very well lit and had a nice little balcony which was adorned with flowers and pink curtains. I got a glimpse of her but then I hid myself. I did not want her to think that I had been waiting for her for an hour. I found a cosy little corner in one part of the park, away from the view of the balcony, and I dozed off.

The sound of thunder woke me. It was very unlike Rajasthan, and particularly this area, to have rains in the month of June. Maybe it was just thunder. I looked up and the first raindrop hit my face, bringing out a small smile. Rain was always welcome in this part of the country. Leave the farmers and the crops, it always helped bring down the temperature a bit.

And then the drops converted to a drizzle, and then to a shower and then it started pouring. And there I was, sitting in the rain, waiting for Radha, for my Radha to come.

As is common with rain in such areas, I saw some sparks and heard a burning sound somewhere. The electricity was out. The dry state of Rajasthan's electricity board had obviously not factored in rain while making the transformers. There was complete darkness all around. The haveli, which was pretty well lit when I had entered, now bore a spooky feel to it.

It then hit me, Radha would not come out in the rain. Something had to be done. I had been thinking about her since the day I had seen her and she had called me to meet her. I could just not let this go. I picked myself up, and I walked towards the back of the haveli. The surrounding fence was around seven feet high with glass splinters on the top. I took my chance.

I had to.

I jumped and caught a portion of the wall which did not have any splinters. I was hanging with one hand on the wall. I tried to look out for a second sweet spot but in the dark it seemed quite difficult. I let my hand free and was back on the ground. She had asked me to meet her at the park behind her house. There had to be an easy way to it. I looked at my watch, 9:45, only fifteen more minutes.

I looked around, nothing came to my head, so I tore one sleeve of my shirt, tied it around the other hand and jumped again. My one hand again got the sweet spot, with no splinters, but this time I used my other hand as well. I let out a cry as a piece of glass tore through the shirt around my hand and ultimately into my skin but my scream got lost within the fury of the rain gods. I picked myself up and very soon was on the other side of the fence. My hand was bleeding profusely and blood mixed with water dripped from my hand. I still had ten minutes. I had to get to her room. I looked around the haveli and figured a way to climb up. It would not be that difficult even with the cut hand.

I managed my way up, the blood loss from my hand had made me kind of dizzy but with 2 minutes left, I was on her balcony. I could see a candle flickering inside. The door was unlocked, I opened it unsure of what to see in front of me.

The room was beautiful. It had pink wallpaper which appeared an even better color in the dim light of the candle. The room was full of photographs and soft toys. Photos of her with her family, with her friends, with her cousins. The bed in the middle of this was like that of a princess, with a net covering it to give it the royal look. The only beautiful thing missing in the room was Radha.

Just then the electricity came back and the lights in the room came on. The beauty of the room was magnified with the additional light but the absence of Radha was now even more stark. It was exactly ten now. I wondered if she had forgotten about what she had said to me. Heartbroken, I turned around to go back, down the balcony and over the glass topped wall again and that is when I saw her, in the park.

She was standing there, exactly at the same spot where I had been some time back, and she was dripping wet. And I was standing in her room, surrounded and guarded by all the soft toys and photographs.

Our eyes met, and even though we were separated by a good 40 metres, and a wall with splinters on it, we knew what this meant. Thunder crackled again, and this time, it brought a smile to both our faces.

We kept on looking at each other for a long time, me in the safe confines of her balcony, with a bleeding hand nevertheless, and she down in the park, which had almost become a pool by now. Just then I heard a sound- "Radha, I hope all is well upstairs."

I did not know what to do, I signalled her to come back and luckily for me she understood. She started running, the smile on both our faces still intact.

The voice spoke again- "Radha, I hope all is well up there." And then after some time, "Radha, where are you Radha?"

And this time I heard footsteps.

I ran and hid under the bed and just then the door opened. Repetition of the same dialogue, "Radha, where are you Radha?"

I could see the boots of the man who I assumed was her father and just then I heard the sweetest voice. "I am here father. In the balcony, enjoying this untimely shower."

I heard the balcony door open and I could see another set of feet, these ones far more beautiful.

"What is wrong with you? You were soaking yourself in the rain outside? You will catch a cold."

"It's ok father. How many times have we seen such rains in our city, and how many times have we seen such a moment in our city. Just wanted to enjoy it while it lasted, and I just wanted to savor the moment."

"Ok. I guess the Gods are very happy with us today. Today is a very special day. You know that it has rained in June after almost 25 years. Today is a very special day indeed."

I heard the voice trailing and the closing of the door and in a lower voice "Yes, today is a very special day."

I pulled myself out from under the bed and there we were, in front of each other, Radha and I.

We did not know what to say for the first few minutes. I was feeling more shy than her and my eyes could not leave the ground. Finally, she spoke. "You came."

"I had to. You had called me."

More awkward looks and more uneasiness. I had scaled a seven foot wall with glass splinters, not even caring about my body once, she had been waiting in the rain, right outside her own house, we both were the least bit scared then, but this moment got the better of us. But being the man, I spoke-" I got you something."

I moved to pick out the little gift from my pocket and she noticed my bleeding hand. She looked at the hand and then looked at me. A tear trickled down her cheeks. She took my hand and led me to the washroom. She tore the piece of shirt around it and put my hand under the cold water. She washed my hand, and I, with my other hand wiped her tears. She opened a cabinet and took out a bandage and some medicine. I tried to stop her but she gave me such a stern look that I just smiled and let her do what she was, all the time with tears in her eyes.

We came back into her bedroom.

"Not the perfect start, I made you cry the first time we met."

"I could not have even dreamt of it being better. And I have been dreaming of this day for quite some time." She looked down, blushing, and the tears still getting the better of her.

I took out a piece of paper from my pocket. "This is for you."

She tried to open it, but the rain had got the better of it.

"What is in it?"

"Something I wrote for you."

"I am impressed! Now tell me what it is."

"Open the paper."

She tried again, but it was too wet. "I have got the poet himself in front of me. Why don't we have a recital."

I had never done such a thing in my life. I had never recited a poem in front of anyone, not even the standard 'Twinkle Twinkle'. But then I had never even written in my life before but when I sat in my hostel room thinking of her, the words just came.

I got up from where I was sitting, bent down on my knee, took her hand in mine, looked her in the eye, and I started

It's not because of the woods
It's not because of the sky
It's not because of the little leaves floating in your chai

It's not because of the light
It's not because of the dark
It's not because of the butterflies flying in the park

It's not because of the wind
It's not because of the glow
It's not because of the raindrops falling with the snow

It's not because of the colours
Red, Green and Blue
The reason that the world is. beautiful
Is You, you.. You!

And the tears started flowing again.

"No one has done any such thing for me ever. Thank you."

I stood up and so did she, and we hugged each other.

We talked a lot that night. She told me about her life. How she had been a protected child. Her father, I came to know, was a very rich and powerful man. He controlled all the village harvest. And he was also a very good man, or that is what she believed. The farmers trusted him blindly to get the best rates for their produce. He also had lots of land and had lots of other small business as well. That is the reason why she was treated a little better than the other girls in college. People respected her father, and were also scared of his strength. Once a guy had made a pass at her in front of her father. The guy was not seen in town after that.

I asked her if her father had killed him, to which she said a very nonchalant yes.

Killing people for honor did not seem a very big thing to her father, or even to her.

That is why people took special care while teasing Radha in

college. Her father had also realised that a little bit of this was part of growing up but she said that if anyone crossed the line, he would meet the same fate as that poor boy.

I had a lump in my throat. I just remembered what I had done with her picture. Thankfully that was under the carpet. Jokingly I asked her what would her father do if he saw me her room with her. She said very simply, "He will kill you."

I was shit scared but her presence somehow soothed the whole thing. We chatted a bit more and she asked me how I landed up in this college. I told her the whole Kota story and the engineering dream. She told me that she had been admitted into a far better college, a Regional Engineering College but her father did not want her to leave town.

We chatted more, about college, about life in general and we did not realise when we fell asleep. I was woken by the first rays of the sun and I looked at her.

The sun rays kissed her cheeks and reached her eyes. She moved and changed direction and her hair fell over her eyes. The sun rays followed her and a gentle breeze blew the hair of her forehead. She looked angelic. She was still in the white kurta and her lips were strawberry pink.

She again changed direction and faced away from me. She could no longer play the game of hide and seek with the sun and sat up. Her eyes still drowsy, but a small smile appearing on her face.

I think that is when I fell in love with her again. She rubbed her eyes and the first thing she saw was me. The smile became wider and then changed to a shriek.

"Aaaaah. What are you doing here. Oh my God. Why haven't you left. If my father sees you, this would be a very premature end to our love story."

I just kept looking at her. This was the first time she had used the word love.

"What is wrong with you? Why don't you understand the gravity of the situation."

And then she looked on the floor.

"Oh my God, there is blood everywhere. I have to clean this and..."

Just then I got up and I kissed her. And she kissed me back, with the same passion. She let go after some time and said "I found heaven"

We both looked into each other's eyes and heard a sound. "Radha, wake up. You have college today."

We heard footsteps.

"Yes father. I am already up. Just getting ready. See you in twenty minutes at the breakfast table. We heard the footsteps retreating.

She had a loving smile on her face and pushed me aside. "Now go."

"But we have twenty minutes. You just said that."

We kissed again and she pushed me again. This time with finality.

"Now go. And there is a small little door on the left hand side. We used to have a dog and had made it for him for easy access to the park behind. Now you use it."

I went to the balcony hiding myself. And then I looked back and said "I will come back."

"Gopal, I wish that you just never go."

I jumped down and easily managed to get out of the haveli and onto the bike.

What a first date!

Time passed by and lots of things were happening in college. Besides studies that is. Our college had a strict zero focus on education. The students did not care about lectures or exams and the teachers cared even less. They used to make guest appearances in the class rooms at times, take attendance, give some general gyaan on what the fuck has happened to the education system in India and how they cannot alone change anything. There would be twenty people listening to them in the beginning but after around five minutes, the number would go down to ten. The strength of the class was around 80 people.

Students found something else to keep them busy. Some discovered new passions in life, like drama, debating, singing or something else and tried to carve a niche there, others- the studious ones who had unfortunately enrolled in our college, but who could not dream to be a part of the student council, started studying for civils so that they could get into administration, some of them started roaming around the city and eve teasing girls for no good reason, and the maximum of the them just slept in the hostel. This would be the way they would pass the next four years. No one would know they existed and they could not care less. And then there were students like me.

Students who had made politics their ultimate aim. I, along with that, also had love to look out for.

College elections were now a couple of weeks away. I tried to be involved in the general meetings, which were open to all, which used to happen in our hostel. We had a pretty huge budget, thanks to the local MLA who used to be part of our hostel, and his party, but still things looked pretty grim. Prithvi was a strong candidate but the issue of the higher number of freshers in the other party had kind of changed the balance. Plus, as a master stroke by Surya, one day back, he had opened the doors of his hostel to the third hostel as well.

The third hostel is something we have not talked much about yet. This was the hostel of all people who were either not of our religion/caste or of the religion/caste of the people in the Gandhi Bhavan. The number of students in the third hostel was not that great and the hostel, with its high Muslim and Dalit population, was now a neglected part of the University. They tried to live in the glory of the past and no one disturbed them in their stupor.

But this time, during the month of Ramazan, Surya had opened the gates of his hostel for them and Id was celebrated in full fanfare in his hostel. All of a sudden, all the students of the third hostel saw him as their leader. It was a master stroke at a master time.

The effect of Surya's largesse was still coming in and Prithvi had more or less conceded defeat. The only ideas that came out of the open discussion we had in our hostel was that we should offer alcohol, the elixir, to the third hostel students.

Prithvi liked the idea. He checked on how much it would cost. The idea brought a faint smile to his otherwise depressed countenance.

But then I told them that Muslims do not savor alcohol.

Prithvi got up, and slapped the person who had given him this idea. Slapped him on his face in front of everyone. And the person he slapped was the vice President of the party and was running for general secretary. "Madar chod. Where the fuck is your brain. Only such rubbish ideas can come to your mother fucking head. Give the Muslims alcohol. You sister fucker, had I done this, we would not have got even a single vote."

The slap pretty much signalled the end of the meeting, and showed the irritation Prithvi was feeling. On losing the election, he would have the huge task of explaining the reason of the loss to the MLA and the usage of the money which had been provided to them. Just then Prithvi turned to me. "And you harami. That day you were saying that no matter what, you will not let Surya win the election. Now what the fuck are you doing except shooting down ideas. You know why we do not win elections. Because stupid people like you happen to be a part of our party. Mother fucker."

Prithvi was shit angry and after his rant on me, he left. And then slowly so did everyone else.

Except me. I sat there thinking what I could do to change the current flavour. What could I do that would make everyone go against Surya. I sat there for 5 hours, thinking of infinite ideas. Our party had a budget which was bigger than theirs, and that is the direction in which I had thought.

I thought that we could capture booths, pay the people who counted the votes, beat people until they voted for us but shot down all these ideas because all these had been thought of, had been deliberated, but had been labelled as not possible to do. It was after all a college election. The police would be covering all this and we did not have *that* much money that we could buy *them*out. There would definitely be gun shots from both sides, some fights and some injuries. But that would be the extent of it. In the 40 years of history of our college, there had been no murders because of the election.

More time passed, a day was now left for the election. I was sitting in Radha's room, I did that once in a week, and was talking love to her, but she could sense the uneasiness. My body was there but my mind was somewhere else.

"Is it the election?"

"What?"

"Gopal, is it the election that is occupying your mind. You have such a beautiful girl lying in front of you, but still, you seem so distracted."

"I guess. In fact, no it's not the election. It's what I had said and have been unable to do."

"What did you say?"

"In the beginning part of college, when we are all ragged, Surya got hold of me and did something that really hurt me. When I got back to my hostel, I told Prithvi, in fact I promised Prithvi, that no matter what, I will not let Surya win the election. And now, no one can stop him from winning."

I paused for a while. My eyes watered but I would not cry in front of Radha.

"Prithvi taunted me the other day. That I can only talk and not do anything else."

I turned away from her, a tear rolled down my cheek.

She spoke.

"Can I do something for you?"

Just then a thought came to my mind. She definitely could do something for me. I turned around.

"No Madam." With the extra stress on the M and the D. And I smiled into her eyes.

"No Madam, such small things keep on happening. I am sure Prithvi did not mean a thing he said. He was just upset that his general secretary candidate had suggested something as stupid as winning over Muslims by giving them alcohol."

She smiled. I continued.

"That would be as stupid as trying to win over Hindus by giving them beef. Leave them Madam. I have such a beautiful girl in front of me. Believe me, the elections are the last thing in my mind right now."

And I kissed her. A long drawn kiss, because the problem which I had been facing for the last few days had been solved. The solution was right in front of me. Only I was blinded, by love, to see it.

I left Radha around midnight, and told her that I would be back the next day. She seemed a little surprised on hearing that as I usually visited once a week but I told her that she helped me distract my mind from the commotion of the elections in the hostel. She said fine, and said that her father was leaving for some other town in the morning for some work and we could probably meet somewhere else as well. She was an only child, she did not have a mother, and when her father went out, no one dared enter her room. This new plan suited me even better and I asked her to meet me near the town lake at 10 pm. She smiled, and said she would be there, not knowing what waited for her.

I rushed back to the hostel. The hostel was a good five kilometres and I had stopped bringing the bike fearing someone might see it parked in a lonely spot once a week and alert Radha's father. I started walking, the speed increased and after some time I was practically sprinting. I covered the five kilometres in nineteen minutes and ran straight into Hari, my best friend's room. I hit the door and it opened with a bang.

Hari was among the group of students who had decided to study for the civils. Even though the IAS and RPSC exams were a good two years away, Hari had devoted more than half of the day studying for them. He helped me maintain a good mixture of thoughts in my life. Whenever he was not studying, he would talk to me regarding the happenings in the world or about history and what learnings one should take from it. Seeing my interest in politics, he would talk to me about different statesmen, kings and politicians.

One story which he had told me a week earlier was about Draupadi, and the role women had played in battles throughout history.

Yudhishtir, the eldest of the pandavas, was the ruler of Indraprastha under the sovereignty of Dhritrashtra. His cousin brother Duryodhana was extremely jealous of the money and respect that the pandavas had earned in the process of developing Indraprastha. Duryodhana wanted the empire to himself and spotted a weakness in the eldest pandava.

Yudishthir was challenged to a game of dice by Duryodhana, his Uncle Shakuni and friend Karna. Shakuni was skilled at the game and was known to win by using unfair means. The plan was that Shakuni would win the empire from Yudhishthir over the game of dice.

The game started and Yudishthir started losing. One by one he lost his wealth and his kingdom. He then put his brothers on stake and lost them as well. He then put himself on stake and lost himself as well. He lost everything he had.

But had he stopped at that, the battle of Mahabharata would probably have never been fought.

Shakuni then prodded him and told him that he had one more thing he could bet, the wife of the five pandavas- Draupadi.

Bhishma and Drona opposed this as a king, no matter how powerful, could not bet a woman, even if she was his own wife, but Yudishthir went ahead. And lost.

Duryodhana ordered his brother Dushasana to bring Draupadi to court. Once there he asked him to take off her sari. Bhima at that moment swore that he would not show his face to his ancestors unless he drank Dushasana's blood and Draupadi swore that she would not tie her hair until she washed them with the same blood.

We all know what happened then as Krishna came as the saviour and Dushasana was unable to disrobe Draupadi. Finally Dhritrashtra's wife came into the court and stopped the disrobing *and in turn granted Draupadi three boons. As the first boon, Draupadi asked for the pandavas to be free from their bondage, as the second boon she asked that all that was lost be returned to Yudishthir.*

When asked for the third boon, she said she is a Kshatriya, and Kshatriyas are given only two boons.

I had understood the role of women in politics and battle only a day before. I banged open Hari's room, looked at him, and smiled.

Hari, lifting his books and wearing his specs-"What's wrong?" On noticing the smile on my face-

"I see the look in your eyes which scares me. What have you done?"

I smiled. "I have done nothing. But I will. Remember the other day you were telling me about Draupadi and her role in the Mahabharata. Today I understood what she did. Today I understood the role of women in the game of politics."

Hari was a little confused. "What happened? Would you please let this politics out of your head. How many times have I told you not to take what Prithvi said seriously. If all those people, with all their money and all their experience and power cannot stop Surya from winning, what the hell can you do? They have tried everything and they have failed. The elections are tomorrow. There is nothing else they can put on line now."

"There is something which they have not put in line yet. They have not used their Draupadi. And unlike the Mahabharata, this time Draupadi will not be lost and stripped. This time, she will change the whole game."

I explained what was in my mind to Hari who could not believe that his best friend had a mind so devious. My initial plan was not to involve anyone but I needed Hari's help in getting this done.

The plan was simple. I would meet Radha, and Hari would be close by. I would kiss her, and then go a little ahead. Hari would click our photos in objectionable positions. We would then threaten Surya that we will circulate these pictures all around the hostel. If this happened, Surya would be defamed because the woman that he loved was with someone else, and that to a fresher from the enemy hostel. No one in this city would vote for a man who could not control his woman. Radha was not Surya's woman, she was my woman, but no one knew that. The whole University knew that Surya loved Radha. We would ask Surya to back out of the elections on the last day, giving Prithvi a straight victory.

The plan was a masterpiece.

And yes, I loved my self esteem more than I loved Radha. I had to deliver on my word. And now I realised that I loved my party even more. A hell lot more. I was willing to make this sacrifice for the party. I was willing to sacrifice my love, my Radha, for the greater good of the party.

Hari quietly listened to every word I said. He had a blank look on his face. I did not know what to make of it. There was complete silence for some time. And then he spoke.

"That day, when you came back for me when we were running away from Gandhi Bhavan. That day I had made a promise to myself, that I will be with you when you need me the most. Without thinking what you are asking me to do, why you are asking me to do. Just this once, I would do anything you would ask me for. No one had ever been with me in the manner you had that day. No one.

Just like you had made a promise of not letting Surya be the President, I had made a promise to be there for you. At least once, or just once, I did not know. But one thing I knew was that if you ever called for me, I would be there for you. I did not know that you will call so soon or for something as repugnant as this. But I knew I would help you."

Tears rolled down his eyes as he said this.

"I now want to know what help of mine you need to get this done."

I looked at my friend and the situation I had put him in. And I silently thanked him for being on my side and for his support. And I now realised that more than his physical support, I needed his mental support to do this.

So I explained him his role. I had to meet Radha at ten and Hari was to get there at 9: 50. His job was to hide and click pictures of both of us.

I would go and give these pictures to Prithvi who would best know how to talk to Surya and get him out of the elections.

The next day passed in anticipation. I arranged for a camera. I did not want to be seen around with one to arouse suspicions when the photographs came so I stole one from the local shop. Hari and I sat quietly in the room. Me, wondering when did this ghost of politics take over my body and Hari, I assume, thinking when did the bond of our friendship become so strong.

We sat in my room for some more time with no words exchanged between us, nothing said at all, and then it was time to go.

Just before we left, Hari said a few lines:

"Between the acting of a dreadful thing
And the first motion, all the interim is
Like a phantasma, or a hideous dream"

"What is that?" I said.

"Having decided that Caesar must die, Brutus reflects on how difficult it is to put his decision into action," replied Hari.

"What?" I said again.

"Another story in history, maybe a time will come when I will tell you about this as well.

We, Hari and I, reached the place where Radha was to come and meet me. It was 8:30 but it was already too dark. I had brought candles and lights to showcase the evening as a special one. We did all the arrangements and by 9: 30 we were ready. Hari hid near the trees and I made myself comfortable. And then in the distance, I saw her silhouette moving.

She came closer and closer and I as I saw her, I thought of cancelling the plan then and there. But I let the thought pass. She was looking beautiful.

She was wearing a red salwar kameez and the red dupatta was tied across her head to hide her face. Only her eyes were visible. Her beautiful big black eyes which hid more than what they gave away, with kajal around them to save her from bad omen. I saw her eyes and saw the love in them, the love for me.

She removed her dupatta and the long tresses unfolded like the waves in the ocean playing to the tune of a flute sung by nature. The hair falling over the face. She moved the hair with her hand and the angelic face came to light. It seemed as if there could be nothing in nature which could be more beautiful than what she was.

She saw me getting lost in her and she smiled. The smile

that lit up the whole world, the special smile which she had reserved only for me, the smile which I had thought about every day since I had seen her, and then she spoke, with the voice which only said love.

"What happened?"

The voice was sexy and seductive. I just nodded my head, first vertically and then horizontally.

"Now come on, I am not looking *that* beautiful. You can now stop staring." She came and sat next to me.

"You are the prettiest girl I have ever seen."

"Hmm. That means you are also checking out other girls." She said this in a playful banter. We both smiled at each other.

I pushed a switch which was behind me, and lanterns, which I had partly immersed in the ground came to light taking a shape of a heart with me and her in between. Hari and I had done this to get perfect lighting for the photographs and had connected the bulbs to a battery. And also, this was the last chance I had to back out. Hari had kept a back out plan, even though I did not want to. If I did not press the switch, the plan would be aborted and Hari would not click any pics. Hari thought that I might change my plans on seeing her, but I knew better. Though I do confess, that I did think of backing out.

Not to forget, the whole thing was crazy romantic.

"Oh my God. This is beautiful. Did you do this?"

I smiled. I pushed on another switch and a table appeared from the ground, I pulled a pulley and a bottle of champagne dropped down from a rope in the tree. I cut the rope and pulled two glasses from behind me.

All she could say was "Oh my God!"

I had to do all this. I had to get her to do more than mere kissing where we had been stuck since the first date. I had to make her feel special. And then I had to use her.

I uncorked the bottle and music started playing. Hari had this time switched the music on and we had correctly assumed that by now she would be feeling too special to notice who was doing what.

I took her hand, and we danced. And as we danced, I said:

As I look back,
To the days that have passed
I wonder how I lived without you
In the past

Since the time I have seen you
Smelt you, felt you
I see no meaning in life
Without you

I never knew,
That my love for someone could be so true
I never knew
Until I met you

And as we now look ahead
To a life of me and you
All I can say right now
Is that I love you

"Happy two month anniversary."

I took out a gold chain, something else I had stolen, and put it around her neck. Her tears just would not stop. She did not say anything, but at such times, eyes do more of the talking.

But only if she could understand what my eyes were saying.

She buried her head into my shoulders, and we swayed to the music. Gradually we kissed, and we lay down. I worked my hands around her clothes, and this time, the magic had worked.

She did not stop me.

After around half an hour we were done. I hoped Hari had taken all the photos. I had to leave and finish the remaining part of the work now but Radha was still lying next to me. But before I could say anything, thankfully, she spoke.

"I love you. Promise me you will never leave my side."

She came towards my side and again buried her head in my chest. I could feel the water of her tears against my body. I knew how much this night had meant to her and how much she had trusted me to let me do what we had done.

I knew how much she had loved me. And I felt so small in front of her.

It's not that I did not love her, it's just that I loved some things more than her. Much much more. So much more that I was willing to sacrifice her honor for those things.

She spoke again.

"I have to leave now. Father's plan changed at the last minute and he is expected back anytime. In fact, that is the reason I had come initially, to tell you that I can't stay. But then, you did all this. You really love me, don't you."

The tears again started falling from her eyes, and then

dripping. I kissed the tears and I nodded my head in agreement. And I said, "I love you."

This was working as per plan. She was leaving, we would now have enough time with the photographs.

Radha left, and I looked at her figure under the moon as she left. Maybe we had meant to be together, but maybe in some other life.

Hari came out of hiding and gave a thumbs up. Although reluctant in the beginning, he had now become an important member of this plan. We cleared up the lanterns and the bottle and threw them in the river. We got on a bike, and headed towards our hostel. Only two words were said in the entire period. "You bastard," said by Hari to me when we boarded the bike. I did not know in what tone he said those words. And I did not really want to know either.

We reached the hostel and went to the internet room. The camera which I had stolen had a memory card. We put the memory card inside the computer and saw the pics. They were perfect. The full face of Radha, and other parts, were completely visible. And so was I. I was about to press the print command when Hari spoke up.

"Wait. We will not show you in the picture."

"Why? We have to threaten Surya that his love is being used by a fresher."

"No. This will reach her father and he will kill you."

"There is no chance this will leave the four walls of the hostel."

"In the last few months, you have been playing the game of politics and I have been studying it. If history has taught us anything, it is that do not trust anyone when it comes to the throne. Even if we remove your face from the pictures, the effect it will have on Surya and his candidature would be the same. Surya will still have to pull out of the election."

His plan made sense. I agreed and we zoomed and took only the pictures where my face was not visible. Hari even suggested that we leave the pictures in front of Prithvi's room and he would know what to do with them. But I wanted to be the hero. I wanted to show Prithvi that I did what I said. I wanted to show him that I was the reason that hostels like ours became legendary. I wanted to show him that I was the future.

Hari excused himself and I went to Prithvi's room. Surprisingly, a night before the elections, he was all alone. He had almost resigned to his fate and there was a bottle of rum in his hand as he gestured me to come in.

"What do you want? Don't you know I have already lost? According to the last analysis, this would be the biggest defeat in the history of this college. Ever."

Instead of drinking from the glass, he took a swig from the bottle.

"Why the hell are you here you mother fucker? Any other grand lines you want to say?"

I replied. "Remember I promised that I would not let Surya win. I am from the Ambedkar Hostel, and at Ambedkar Hostel, we are men. We fulfil our promises."

Prithvi got up on his back. All of a sudden the alcohol had zero affect on him.

"What can you do now?"

I handed him the envelope I was carrying. The envelope which carried the pictures.

He opened them, and his eyes did not even blink once. I started speaking.

"We can take these pictures to Surya and ask him to step out of the elections. Otherwise, we will circulate these pictures all over the University and he will not be able to show face ever."

Prithvi was studying the pictures very closely and asked me. "I have two questions. Promise me you won't lie."

"I promise."

"Ambedkar Bhavan promise?"

"Ambedkar Bhavan promise."

"Is the guy you in the picture? And if it is you, who else knows this?"

This was Prithvi, I had nothing to be scared off.

"Yes this is me. Hari, me and obviously Radha know that this is me."

"No one else?"

"No one else."

"Are you sure?"

"Yes."

"Do you trust Hari?"

A smile came on my face. "More than I trust myself."

"Okay, good. Now destroy the camera, the computer, or anything which has any proof that this is you. Don't worry, you will be suitably rewarded. You have done great service to your hostel. I have bigger plans than what you thought of about these pictures. I am proud of you. In you, I see a President of the University"

The last sentence made the deception of Radha worth it. "Thank you sir."

"Now leave. And make sure no one sees you leaving. I have got lots of work to do."

What happened after that is what I could not have even imagined in a 100 years.

Prithvi, after getting the photographs from me, did not go to Surya to force him to quit the election. He went to the Xerox shop and got more than a thousand copies photo copied. He then called an emergency meeting of the entire second and third year hostellers and distributed the leaflets amongst them, to be plastered on any and every wall of the University and town. Prithvi had declared out and out war. He was not playing for this election, he could have easily taken the pictures to Surya and won the election, he was playing it for eternity. He wanted to eradicate the Gandhi Bhavan might, once and for all.

So as I slept in my room, pictures of me and my love Radha were being seen by everyone. Such things are very easy to spread, within a couple of hours the whole world was talking about the pictures. I heard a murmur around me and the noise awakened me. There was something happening in the hostel. I came out and saw complete chaos. Students from our hostel were running around all over with posters in their hands. I stopped one of the seniors and saw the paper. Yes, it was Radha, and it was me. All hell broke loose and I fell to the ground.

I was awakened by some water being sprayed on my head. Hari had thrown some water on me and I regained consciousness.

"Hari, what happened? What happened with the photographs?"

"Gopal, an hour back, Prithvi ordered to have the photographs plastered all over town. Every Tom, Dick and Harry of the town would have seen them by now. He had initially copied a 1000 copies but that number has multiplied manifolds. Everyone has seen them, everyone."

"But what about me? Have they figured the person in the photograph is me?"

Hari was a little taken aback by the question. I think he would have thought that I would be a little more concerned about Radha as everyone had seen her in the compromising position. He replied- "No, I don't think people will figure out it was you." He pulled a sheet of paper from his back pocket. It was the photo, and on it was written

Surya and Radha caught.
This is how he will treat your sisters.

Not very creative lines but that was the least of my concerns. Prithvi had completely changed the game. He had branded Surya as the guy in the photo. Everyone knew that Surya had a crush on Radha, so believing what had been written would be very easy for everyone. Plus, it was a day before the elections, no one would have the time or energy to find out the truth before the polls were conducted. And as I said earlier, in these parts, you might tease girls, you might talk dirty about them, but you never, you never disrespected them the way it had been done, supposedly by Surya. You never made public you most private moments.

And this was a blow which would hit not only the current elections, but Gandhi Bhavan would take an eon to get over this deathly blow. A blow, which had been made true partly by me, and partly by the genius political brain of Prithvi. It was now my turn to show my genius.

I grabbed the paper and rushed to the toilet. I wet my face, opened my eyes wide and put water in them so that they would turn red. After completing my make up I went towards Prithvi's room. Prithvi was still there. Hari had followed me behind.

"Why did you do this?" I knew the answer but I still asked him. The countenance that I was carrying made me look like a person who had lost in love.

"I did this for the greater good. You will not understand."

I tried to fake some tears and said in a sombre voice, "Try me."

"Had I given the photos to Surya, we would have won this election. But by doing what I did, I have assured victory for ever."

He was saying exactly what I had thought he would. He continued.

"Today, I have finished the Gandhi Bhavan- for ever."

"And my love?"

"It was a sacrifice I was willing to make."

He did not know that that was a sacrifice which even I was willing to make.

"Did you never think of me? Not even once?"

"I did. But as I said, it was for the greater good. Tell me what you want? I will not say no to anything."

This was the reason I was here. This was the reason I had pretended to be distraught in front of him, this was the reason I was willing to sacrifice Radha and her love. I had to play this very smart.

"I want a position in the council."

"You are only in the first year!"

"I want a position in the council."

"Granted."

I covered my face, and I walked away. Hari followed behind. Little did Prithvi know that I had covered my face to suppress the smile, not the sadness.

Hari and I walked quietly towards my room and we entered. Hari closed the door behind me and we were face to face. I smiled and opened my arms to embrace him when he gave me a tight slap. Right on the face.

"You do not care about anyone, do you? What did that poor girl do to you to deserve this?"

The smile returned on my face. Hari slapped me once more.

"What the fuck is wrong with you? Where is my friend who I have loved for the past few months? What have you become?"

"I have become a part of the council. No one in the history of the University had managed that in the first year. That is what I have become."

"So politics is so important to you now that you can give

away your love for it? What if one day comes that you have to chose between me and politics. What will you chose then?"

"Don't make me say something you will not like to hear."

Hari just stood there and stared at me. He walked out of the door and slammed it shut. I knew he would come around in a few days. Who wouldn't? Who wouldn't want to be the best friend of a member of the student council?

I lay down on the bed and slept off with a satisfied smile on my face. The road to be the President in three years had become much easier. There was no way in hell anyone could even think of challenging me now.

I slept the soundest sleep ever. Not knowing what was happening elsewhere, to Radha, to Surya. In fact, not caring what was happening elsewhere.

The rays of the sun entered my room around 7 am but the kind of sleep I was in, I slept till around 9. The elections were to start in around an hour's time. I came out of my room to see what had happened over night.

I opened the door and there seemed to be a quiet celebration. Sweets were being offered to everyone but not in the boisterous manner you would associate with our hostel. I asked one of the guys what was happening.

"What happened? Why are you distributing sweets before the elections have even started?"

"Don't you know, Gandhi Bhavan has withdrawn from the election."

I smiled. He did not know the reason behind the withdrawal. The reason was standing right in front of him.

"Why did they withdraw? Because of the leaked photos?"

"You don't know anything is it?"

He said this and walked away. I got hold of him and asked him again.

"What happened, will you tell me?"

"Radha's father killed Surya and Radha. Her body was found in her bedroom and Surya's body in his hostel. Her father surrendered to police after that. Where have you been all this while?"

I was stunned. The news hit me like a bullet and I started shivering. I lost control over my arms and legs, blood seemed to be flowing in every part of my body and it seemed as if it would burst out. Please someone tell me this was not true. Please someone tell me this was a nightmare. Please someone get me out of this.

And I fainted, in front of my room, for the second time in two days.

When my eyes opened, I was back in my room. Hari was sprinkling water over me.

"Wake up. Are you okay? Wake up."

I woke up with a startle.

"Hari, please tell me all that I heard is false. Please tell me they did not do anything to Radha. Please Hari, please. I do not want to be a killer Hari. Please Hari. Please."

Hari did not slap me this time. He just hugged me. And that was the moment when the answer to the question he had asked me earlier changed. If I had to chose between him and politics, I would chose him.

The next few days passed very quietly. Our party obviously had a thumping victory. The Gandhi Bhavan did not vote, and the third candidate was no match to Prithvi. The celebrations were kept low key and I was inducted into the student council as a Deputy General Secretary.

As the days passed, I got over the guilt of the two murders that had been committed by me. I got engrossed in the everyday running of the University and as they say, power corrupts, absolute power corrupts absolutely.

I was over the murders, I had a lifetime in front of me. A lifetime of politics.

HARI'S STORY

I was running frantically and Gopal was running with me. My almost bald head, a result of the on-going ragging, a stark comparison to the wavy tresses Gopal was carrying around. I was almost jealous of the kind of confidence he exuberated. While the entire hostel had to go to the barber under the mango tree to get their hair set in the freshers style, this guy had somehow managed to pull a coup and no one said anything to him about the way he kept his hair. I also wanted long hair, but as many things in life with me, I knew that this would also be a wish unfulfilled.

A stone was thrown towards Gopal. He had not looked back for even a single moment since we had started running. The stone almost kissed his hair and for the first time he looked back at who had thrown the stone. I think he made a mental note to get back at that person. But now was not the time. We kept on running.

The market was as crowded as you would expect in a city as big as where we were. The lanes were not that wide but were full of hawkers, shopkeepers, people who had come to shop, people who were just there and Gopal and I, who were running for dear life. Just then we saw a scooter in front of us. Gopal looked at me and I looked back at him. In an instant we knew what had to be done. I think that was the moment when our friendship started. Both of us were now on either side of the scooter and we pulled the man riding the scooter down. It was the first time I had physically hurt someone. The scooter now occupied the by lane in entirety and the little man was under it. It helped us get a little ahead of the pack that was following us.

We ran more. We ran faster.

Just when we thought we had lost them, the guilt of hurting an unsuspecting and unwilling participant of this chase hit me and I looked back to see how the person we had just pulled down was doing.

When I turned back, I could not see that person but what I could see was a stone headed right towards me. I forgot all about the scooter guy and on an impulse, swerved to the right and hit a person on a bicycle, taking him down with me. Now there were two unwilling sacrifices to this chase.

I lay there, in between all the rubble of the broken bicycle and the owner of the bicycle, who had been smarter than me and had run off seeing the bunch of guys running after me.

I lay there, all alone, waiting for death to come to me. Gopal had managed to give them the slip and would now be victorious and on the way to our hostel. And I lay there in the middle of the road, waiting for my predators. I touched my head and felt something liquid, I looked at my hand and it was blood. In the fear of the impending beating, I had forgotten what had hit me. The stone, which I had tried to evade had landed on my forehead and blood was gushing out of it. But that seemed to be the lesser of the concerns as I saw the Gandhi Bhavan seniors rushing towards me.

There were around ten of them. They saw me lie there and a smile appeared on their faces.

One of them shouted to the others.

"We have got one, the other bastard would be around here someone."

And then I don't know why, but I spoke. "You will never get him, he has already gone back. You will never be able to catch him."

I got a kick on my gut for my outlandish behaviour. A tear trickled down my eyes, and before I could wipe it off, the enemy seniors saw it.

They all started laughing looking at me.

"We should make an example of him so that the bloody Ambedkar Bhavan knows where its place is. In shit."

"Let's show them what kind of ragging we do at Gandhi Bhavan. We will get him ragged by our freshers."

A fresher getting ragged by another fresher was the biggest insult that a person could take in our college.

"We will keep him in the dark room of our hostel and will not let him go out of the hostel for 2 days with no water or food."

"We will bloody strip him naked and leave him in the girl's hostel."

I believed all they had said and the single tear now became a flow. My scared countenance gave fuel to their fire and they scared me more and hit me more. All I could do in the meanwhile was cry my heart out, and wait for some divine intervention. And divine intervention did come in the form of Gopal.

But I really don't know what was in his mind. Instead of coming to the scene on his knees begging for forgiveness, he came charging in towards the group. I thought maybe he had something in his mind, or maybe he had been successful in getting some backup, but all my thoughts and hopes went crashing with him when a senior in front of the person he was charging, saw him, picked him and pinned him- on me.

The divine intervention had already led to much more pain and I could not even imagine what would be in store for us when we were taken back to Gandhi Bhavan.

A few months and an election later

Gopal was the most ambitious person I had ever known in my life. He had practically sacrificed two lives to get into the student council, out of which one was the girl he had loved. And I unwittingly, or that is what I would like to believe, had been a part of his rise. And he also ensured that I got my due.

The celebrations, and activities, following the elections were pretty low key, maybe as a sign of respect for the deceased. But gradually things fell into place.

One day, almost three months after the elections and after Gopal had been the first first year student to be included in the council, we were sitting in Gopal's room.

"Hari, it's been two months since I became the Deputy General Secretary. I don't think I have actually done much in this period."

"It's been three."

"What?"

""It's been three months since you assumed the post, the 'deputy general secretary', and you have done as much as any first year student can do. But the fact of the matter is, that our party has seemed to lost focus. It is the seniors who are actually not up to anything constructive. They are just basking in the glory of their victory and making the juniors do all the work. That is fine, we are doing it, but obviously they have not entrusted any big responsibility on us yet. It's only the small things which are getting done. The more important things, the onus of which lies on them, nothing is being done in that regard. If anything, the Gandhi Bhavan folks are trying to win back their lost glory by trying to get sympathy for the slain Surya. A long shot it is, as no one in the University will sympathise with someone who leaked a girl's naked pictures, but still, at least they are trying something. But again, as I said, why are you singling yourself out. Prithvi has still not been able to get over the fact that he won and is immersed in alcohol the whole day. The remaining council just feels that if he is not taking the initiative, why should they?"

"You are right. They have absolutely nothing to gain. Outside the University, the only person who commands respect in the political circles is the President, and if that fucker doesn't give a damn, then honestly, nobody cares about the rest. But you know the difference between the rest of the council and me? They will slip into oblivion next year. Maybe take some petty jobs, or maybe try and get through the civils like you are. But I, I will have to face the people of our University again for elections next year. And if things go the way they are at present, I don't see myself getting any position next year."

There was some silence as we both dawned on what the outcome would be if such a thing occurred. Though the early seat in the council was a great thing for Gopal, it also put him under enormous pressure of regaining that position every year till he could fight for the post of the President. If even for one year he could not find a place in the council, his political ambitions would take a huge beating. He spoke up again.

"Hari, think of something. We cannot let this golden opportunity slip away from our hands. I am a member of the council in the first year. You realise how big a thing that is! We have to capitalise on it. We have to make it work for us."

I smiled in my head as Gopal said these lines. After the Radha and Surya episode, our friendship had reached a new level altogether. Nowadays, whenever Gopal talked about something, it always used to be about 'us' rather than only about 'him'. It gave me a sort of confidence to know that someone as strong and important as him was on my side and was my best friend.

I suppressed the smile and spoke back.

"Gopal, let us think over this. I don't think the solution can come in one conversation. Let's both sleep over it and let's talk about this tomorrow."

That was the end of that conversation. We then talked about some general happenings. He asked me how my preparation for my civil exams was going, I said pretty good. We then talked about movies and cricket and he mentioned how Radha had a huge television in her room where he had once seen a cricket match with her. The name of Radha kept on propping up in our conversations from time to time. I don't think either of us had forgotten what had happened to of her. Gopal wanted to use her as a tool, but he never, he never wanted her to be killed. In fact, once, under the influence of alcohol he had told me that he had plans of marrying her. That he had imagined things would go the way he had planned. That Prithvi would show the photos to Surya who would then step down from the elections. No one would get to know or see those pictures and his love affair with Radha would continue and they would eventually get married and have kids.

Maybe he was naive, or maybe he was new at this game of politics. The truth still remained that we had killed her. The good part was no one except Prithvi knew who the person in the photo was. We did not need forgiveness from the world. We needed forgiveness from ourselves, and I guess, over time we would get that.

I slept over in Gopal's room and when I was woken up, Gopal was all ready and was full of excitement.

"Get up you bastard, I have got the brilliant plan."

"What time is it?"

"How does that matter? It's five. Now shut up and get up and listen to my plan."

I got up from the bed rubbing my eyes and saw a lit up face of Gopal. He had taken my suggestion figuratively and not literally. He had actually thought about what had to be done in order to consolidate his position in the party and in the University.

"Ok, what?"

Gopal took a glass of water and emptied it over my head. I woke up with a startle.

"What the hell is wrong with you?"

"I need your full attention. So now listen."

And he told me his plan.

The plan was pretty simple. Our University had a cultural fest. He, being the deputy general secretary, would definitely have a role to play in it. The fest was an average fest in which participation was generally from within our own University because the budgets were low and hence the prizes were low. Honestly speaking, no one really cared about our fest. And that is what Gopal wanted to change.

"Hari, I will make our fest the most talked about event in this part of the country. I will invite famous singers, I will increase the prize money so that colleges from Delhi University also take part. Just imagine, colleges from Delhi University coming all the way to our college, for the grand prize. I will organise a sports festival along with that. Even the timing is perfect, it is December, when the weather is perfect for playing. I will make the fest the biggest thing our little town has seen."

The plan was pretty good. Gopal was looking at me with his huge eyes expecting a revert. I spoke.

"Hmmm. I think the plan is pretty good. Just some small issues which I have. I haven't thought this through but these are the issues I can see right up."

The smile on Gopal's face somewhat faded. "Tell me, what problems do you foresee."

"See, Gopal, I think this is not the first time someone

would have thought of this. One big reason that our college fest is not that great is because we just don't have the budgets. Everything you have said- grand prize money, famous artists to perform, sports tournament etc. Everything needs a lot of money. And our University does not have that kind of money. Most of the colleges which host such big events get their money from sponsors and where will we get any sponsors from? Who will want to invest so much money in a college like ours?"

Gopal had a smile the entire time I was speaking. He had already thought about this issue and I knew he had a solution to it. I just did not know what. And I wanted to know what his devious mind had thought.

"Hari, when I was with Radha, there were a lot of other things we did besides what you had captured on your camera. We also talked, and talked a lot. She was the only daughter of a very very important and rich man who besides being rich and important, also had lots of rich and important enemies. Her father was always living under the fear that he would one day be killed and all his property and money would be taken by his blood hungry relatives and enemies and nothing would be left for his poor daughter. So you know what he had done, he had stashed a hell amount of gold in a secret place for her so that if such a situation ever came, she could take the gold and run away. No one would care where she went as long as she did not take their money, and no one knew about the gold. It was a brilliant plan, more so because the value of the gold which he hid also kept on increasing as the time went by."

Gopal still had the smile on his face. More than a smile, it was a smirk. He had definitely forgiven himself for doing what he had done to Radha. I guess it was high time that I did too. He continued.

"We had planned, and in the brief period we were together, we had even considered that both of us will take the gold and run away. She had told me that her father would never agree to her marrying a person from a different community. She had wanted to run away with me a month after we had met but I asked her to wait. I asked her to wait for at least 6 months, until her eighteenth birthday. And mind you, I was pretty serious about her myself and had decided that we actually will run away. But who knew what fate had in store for us. Her father killed her and then Surya. The gold was obviously the last thing on his mind at that time, so basically, he left all the gold for me. The person in the picture with his daughter for which he had killed someone else."

Gopal had a smile on his face. He could do anything for politics. He was going to use Radha again for his personal gains.

I just nodded. He continued.

"And yes Hari, I do know where the gold is hidden. So my dear friend, the first problem which you had envisioned has been taken care of. Now tell me, do you see any other issue."

I tried to divert my mind from Radha and what we had done to her. If he had forgiven himself for what he had done, and was now even planning to use her money, I guess I could very easily forgive myself as well. Gopal on not getting any response asked me again.

"So tell me, what other issue do you envision?"

"Gopal, honestly speaking, I think this is a brilliant plan."

The smile on his face grew bigger. He did value my opinion a lot.

"I think this is a brilliant plan. Obviously you know how much gold is there in hiding and obviously you have done your calculations."

"Brother, it is a hell lot of money. I would only be taking a drop from the sea."

"Okay, so the money is sufficient, and I bet that you will be able to pull this off. My only concern is that even the seniors would have thought of making the college fest a big deal. Believe me, there is lots of money to be pocketed when the college fest is big. So even the seniors would have thought of this, and once they see an inflow of money in this, they will take over the reins from you and you will not be able to do anything. First of all, they will ask you for the origin of this money."

"That's easy. I will tell them I got it from some random company in Delhi. Believe me, once they see the money they will not even want to double check."

"That's fine. But my thinking is that once the money enters the University, they will take charge of all the decisions and your name will be lost in the long list of students vying for recognition. Obviously, they will give you a carrot, which I think in this case would be money, but then, all the money would be yours so the carrot will not make any sense!"

The smile which Gopal was carrying went down a bit.

"So are you telling me that we should not do this?"

"Are you out of your mind? Obviously we will do this. But we will directly go and tell Prithvi that we have managed to get sponsors. That will help in your candidature for the next year elections at least. The fest will not make you an overnight favourite, but it will greatly help your cause."

The smile somewhat returned on Gopal's face.

"So basically you are telling me that we have to do this, but doing this is not enough."

"Exactly. The fest is something that has been happening for years. What will really help our cause is if we can think of something which has not been thought of yet and convert that into something huge. But honestly, I think if we are able to pull off this fest for this year, we will be safe at least for next year. We will then have to think of something new as a good fest next year would be something which everyone will take for granted."

"And the thought process for that starts the next year."

"Correct."

I dozed off for some more time and Gopal booked an appointment with Prithvi to discuss his plans for the fest. The meeting went as I thought it would go.

Prithvi: "So what brings you here?"

Gopal: "Sir, I had some plans which will help us build a name for our University."

Prithvi: "How will it help me and my party?"

Prithvi was known to be blunt with his answers.

Gopal: "Sir, what I had done last time led us to win the elections. You know how good my plans and their execution is."

Prithvi: "Now don't start flying. Quickly tell me what the plan is. I have other work to pay heed to."

His other work consisted of a bottle of rum and cola.

Gopal: "Sir, we have one of the worst fests."

Prithvi: "Are you telling me or are you asking me?"

Gopal: "Sir, I am telling you. From what I have heard, nothing actually happens during the fest. No one really cares about it."

Prithvi: "And you want to change that?"

Gopal: "Yes sir."

Prithvi: "And may I ask you why?"

Gopal: "Sir to make our University famous."

Prithvi: "You are wasting my time."

Gopal had to talk Prithvi's language. And Prithvi's language was him and his party.

Gopal: "Sir, if we have a big budget for the fest, we can utilise it in the manner we want. I hope you get what I mean."

Prithvi obviously got what he meant. Gopal later told me that he thought that for a leader Prithvi was very near sighted. Looking for immediate gains rather than how a good fest would help us become popular amongst the students who would keep on voting for us. I reminded him that this was Prithvi's last year and unlike us, he did not care for future elections.

Prithvi: "Don't tell me you think that no one has ever tried to get a budget for our fest. How on earth will you manage it?"

Gopal smiled. Prithvi had bought into the plan at least.

Gopal: "Sir, you don't worry about that. I will make sure that our college fest has the biggest budget."

Prithvi: "If you can pull this off, great. I will give you a good percentage of the total amount."

Gopal was bargaining for a percentage of his own money. Not exactly his own, but the whereabouts of which were known only to him in the free world, so the money was practically his.

Gopal: "Sir, I don't want a big cut. All I want is involvement in organising the fest."

Prithi: "That's even better. Now go. I give you two weeks to get the money. Otherwise we do the usual. Take the money from the University, keep more than half of it, and do a small little *mela*. Because honestly, this plan has been tabled infinite times and no one has ever managed a sponsor for our shitty University."

Gopal: "But I have proven myself before."

Prithvi: "And that is why you get this chance. Now go."

Gopal came back to his room and I was waiting for him. He could not control his excitement and wanted to go and get the money right then. I cooled him down and asked him what happened. He told me the whole story.

I told him that we will go to Prithvi with the money, but after three weeks. Gopal asked me why.

I told him that Prithvi was obviously a very smart political brain. It might not appear so but that was why he was selected as the Presidential candidate for our hostel. If we went to him a day later with truck loads of money he would suspect something fishy. We would wait for him to forget about this conversation and would then take the money to him. A week more than the time he gave us did not matter as long as we got the money. And for the major part of these three weeks, we would be underground, not visible to anyone so that when the money came, we could tell them that in the periods we went missing, we were actually in Delhi trying to arrange for the money.

Gopal agreed. He had to, the plan made complete sense. But he wanted to get the gold out of the hiding spot because selling it would also be an issue. We would have to sell it in small amounts and that to in different towns and villages so that people would not suspect us. We thought what a good budget would be and decided on Rs. 25 lacs. The real budget for last year's fest had been Rs. 2 lacs out of which only Rs. 50,000 was used for the purpose of the fest.

Gopal took me with him when he went to take out the gold. I asked him what the worth of the gold would be and what he would do with the rest of it. He told me that Radha had told him that it would be worth nearly Rs. 2 crore. I was shocked to hear the amount. Gopal really should have run away with Radha with that much money and I told him so. He would never be able to earn that much money ever in his life.

And then Gopal told me that he saw this Rs. 25 lacs as an investment. An investment to a life in politics where he would make much much more than what Radha's father could have ever hidden.

We waited for the night and set off.

We reached Radha's house and I was kind of surprised that the place of hiding was so close to where she had lived. And all the fears of Radha's father had actually come true. As soon as he was incarcerated for the double murder, his relatives had started fighting amongst themselves for that extra bit of money. Luckily, no one knew where the 2 crore rupees were hid. No one except Gopal.

We reached the park behind Radha's house. Gopal moved towards a bench, looked around and started working near the leg of the bench.

"What are you doing Gopal? Is this the place where the gold was hid?"

"No, not here. If everything Radha told me was correct, then the leg of this bench has a key to the safe in which the gold is hidden."

Gopal kept on fiddling with the bench until we both heard a click. The leg of the bench opened and out came a bunch of keys.

Gopal looked at me, gave me a thumbs up, and we set off again.

The plan made by Radha's father was pretty simple. Hide the key at one place and the gold in a safe in some other place. Someone had to know about both in order to get the gold. And that someone could only be Radha. Or that is what he had assumed.

Gopal rode our bike out of the town and onto the highway. We stopped near a milestone which read – Delhi 313 km.

"This is it. This is where the money is hid."

"Where? Under this milestone?"

"I am not sure but it is here somewhere. When Radha was about to tell me where exactly it was, we both heard a sound and I had to run and hide. It turned out to be nobody but the moment was lost."

"So you do not know where exactly it is?"

"I know it is here somewhere. You have the shovels right."

"Right."

"So let's start digging."

We both started digging and did so for around half an hour. Nothing had showed up. The milestone was now practically out of the ground and we had dug for around a metre but had nothing to show for it.

We dug for half an hour more but again nothing. Then an hour more but still nothing.

We both sat up with our backs to each other. Gopal spoke in disappointment.

"So I guess we will have to think of the other plan before next year. Where the fuck did that bastard keep the gold. And why the fuck did she not tell me? And how the fuck did he think she could dig all this?"

Just then it struck me. He had hid the gold for his *daughter.* A daughter who was pretty but not strong by any stretch of the imagination. The money had to be right in front of us. Some place which *she* could access very easily, and that too alone.

I stood up.

"I know where the money is."

"Where?"

I looked at the milestone and Gopal knew what I meant. We hit the milestone with the shovel and realised it was not made of normal cement. We hit it a couple of times more and a small hole appeared. We looked at the bunch of keys we had and one fit perfectly into it.

We had the gold.

We took out all the gold, which was in the form of mainly biscuits and were ready to make a move when suddenly we saw a jeep approaching us. It was the police. How the hell did they get to know what was happening?

Under normal circumstances we would have just stayed there and they would have passed. But we had 2 crore worth of gold with us and we did not want to take chances. We got on our bike but it refused to start. We had to think, and we had to think fast. We had dug up a good bit of ground and they police was definitely going to question us.

Just then Gopal gave me the 2 crore gold and asked me to hide in the bushes. He said he would take care.

The whole thing took me by surprise and I asked him "Do you trust me with this much money?"

"I trust you more than my life. And if you betray me, nothing would be worth living for. Not even the post of the President."

We had indeed come a long way.

So I hid in the bushes and the police approached. Gopal acted drunk. One constable came out.

"Who the hell do you think you are and what are you doing here? And why have you dug up this whole place?"

Gopal replied, in a drunk tone. "I am the deputy general secretary of the University and I can do anything I want."

And he slapped the constable.

The constable could not believe what had just happened. He had been slapped by a n*ormal* person. Such things did not happen in the city we lived in. The constable slapped him back, twice. Gopal smiled because the plan was working. The attention of the constable was diverted from the dug up ground to Gopal. And I was safely hiding with 2 crores worth of gold in a bush nearby.

The constable handcuffed him and put him in the jeep. Gopal knew it was going to be easy for him to get free. He was after all not a *normal* person. He was the deputy general secretary.

And the gold was safe, with me.

As was decided, the next three weeks were spent by me and Gopal travelling from town to town and selling gold in bits. We lived a nice luxurious life for the next three weeks staying at the best hotels and eating the best food and drinking the best wine and mingling with the best girls. This was the life Gopal had wanted to live, and this was the life Gopal would live once he became the President of our University and then went on to become bigger and better in the game of politics.

We had initially thought that we would convert the entire amount to cash but then thought against it. While coming back, we hid a good chunk of it again in the outskirts of our city with both of us having a key and both keys being necessary to get to the gold.

I realised that Gopal had shared half of his fortune with me. Something which he did not really have to do.

We came back to our city after three weeks. And nothing had changed. No activity took place in the college and nobody cared. As soon as we reached, Gopal went to Prithvi and this time he also took me along. I asked him why as I was never involved in such things. Gopal said that he would tell me later.

Prithvi: "So you again. Aren't your two weeks over yet?"

Gopal: "I took one week more. But I have not come back empty handed."

Prithvi: "So what have you got? How much money have you managed from the sponsors?"

Gopal (in a very low tone): "We spent the last few weeks in Delhi. And now we are back. We have managed to get twenty five."

Prithvi started laughing.

"Hahaha. Twenty five thousand in 3 weeks! I really can't understand how I will spend this money? Wait, what did you want, you wanted a decision making role in this fest right. You wanted to organise this fest right? I will make you the organising head and I give you twenty five thousand more. How many did I say? Twenty five thousand more for a grand total of fifty thousand rupees. Now go and organise this fest you mother fucking asshole."

His tone had changed from playful to outright mean. Maybe it was the rum and cola talking or maybe it was the disappointment. Maybe on some level he did expect Gopal to get the money. Gopal was the sole reason he had won the elections. Gopal and I.

Gopal: "Sir, by twenty five I meant Twenty five lacs. And thank you for making me the organising committee head."

Prithvi could not speak. The alcohol which he had been consuming for the last few months all of a sudden had no effect on him anymore. His jaw dropped, his eyes almost blew out and I bet if I had concentrated a bit more, I could have seen smoke coming out from his ears.

Gopal had given him a knock out punch.

Prithvi: "How much money did you say you have?"

Gopal: "Twenty five lacs sir. And I think I can do a brilliant fest in the amount which I have."

Prithvi rushed to his door and closed it behind him. The alcohol had completely left his body by now. He faced Gopal and started speaking in a very fast tone.

"So listen to me very carefully now. And whatever we talk about now, remains between these four walls. We have kept our secrets before and it has benefitted all of us."

He looked at Gopal and Gopal nodded his head. He then looked at me and I also followed suit.

"So whatever I say, stays within these four walls. You have twenty five lac rupees. How many people know about this so far?"

Gopal: "Well, me, Hari and now you." And then as an afterthought, "And the company which has given me this money."

Prithvi: "Very nice. And this information will stay privy to the three of us only. We will manage the sponsor company by showing him fake invoices. I will manage that, you don't worry."

Prithvi was thinking of something in his head. He continued.

"So what we will do is, we will tell the entire party that we have received only 10 lacs."

Gopal: "Only ten?"

Prithvi: "Ok twelve, but nothing more than that. You give me the remaining amount and I will know the best use for it then. I will use it for the party."

Gopal: "Oh just fuck off!"

A chill went down my spine. I was stunned at the audacity which Gopal had shown. Had he just asked the President of our University to fuck off! I tried to do something smart and I intervened.

"No Gopal, I will not fuck off. I had a hand in getting this money as well and I most certainly will not fuck off."

Both of them turned towards me. Surprised as to how did I come into the conversation all of a sudden. I did not know what to say, they were both looking at me expectantly. I had just said that so that Gopal had some time to think to save his ass. He had said something in the heat of the moment and I knew he would repent this later. I just wanted to give him some time so that he could correct himself. But they both were looking at me and were expecting me to say something. So I just repeated what I had said earlier.

"No Gopal, I will not fuck off. I had a hand in getting this money as well and I most certainly will not fuck off."

Gopal looked at me and I almost evoked a smile from him in this awful moment.

Gopal: "No Hari, I did not ask you to fuck off. I asked this mother fucking bastard Prithvi to fuck off."

He then looked at Prithvi and said again. "Fuck off."

Even Prithvi did not know what had hit him. He had never been talked to in this tone. Gopal continued.

"You think I do not know what you will do with this money. You will bloody take it and splurge it on this whiskey, girls, and maybe a new car for yourself."

Prithvi still could not believe what was happening to him. Gopal continued.

"And please for heaven's sake, start drinking a better brand of wine. And please start smoking a cigarette and leave this *bidi*. You carry around our reputation and this is not the way I want it seen."

No one spoke a word for the next few minutes. But I could hear my heart beat as if AK 47s were being fired.

Finally, Prithvi spoke up.

"Ok, so what do you want? Do you want a part of the money?"

Gopal: "You idiot, if I wanted a *part of the money*, I could have had the whole amount of the money. Remember, it is I who got you the money."

Prithvi had a stupid look on his face,

Gopal: "So what I want is two things. I want to be the head of the organising committee."

Pritvhi: "Done."

Gopal: "And next year, I want to be included in the council again. I will organise such a fest that there is no chance we will not win the elections again."

Prithvi: "Done."

Gopal: "And you mother fucker can have all the money you want. We do not want the cut. And yes, there is a third thing."

Prithvi: "What?"

Gopal: "Never dare call me a mother fucker again."

Gopal said this and opened the door to Prithvi's room and left. I did not want to look at Prithvi and I also quietly marched off after a moment of awkward silence.

Gopal and I did not speak a word till we reached his room. Gopal slammed the door shut and after all this while he looked at me. A little smile came on his face, which then gradually turned into full blown laughter. He mimicked me and said.

"No Gopal, I will not fuck off. I had a hand in getting this money as well and I most certainly will not fuck off."

And then we both started laughing like crazy. He had just insulted the President of the University. He had all the right to do anything he wanted. After around five minutes, when we could laugh no more, I spoke.

"There are so many questions that I do not even know where to start from."

Gopal: *"No Gopal, I will not fuck off....."*

Me: "Shut up and listen to me. When did, okay why did you do this? When did you decide to do this? Didn't you think that Prithvi would, I don't know, maybe kill you?"

Gopal maintained the smile on his face. "He is a spineless motherfucker. And you know when I decided to have a go at him? When he said that don't tell anyone about the money."

Me: "Why? We always knew he would keep the money for himself."

Gopal: "No. You thought he would keep the money with himself. I thought he would put it back into the party."

Me: "What difference does it make?"

Gopal: "Hari my friend, you might read all you want to in books about history. But there are very few things which I have understood in life. But I have understood them well. Very well. Today, when he said he wanted the money for himself, I remembered a story my father had told me when I was a little kid. I guess even your father would have told it to you. And I bet he would have told you a lot more stories. But the difference is that I did not hear the story, I understood it."

Me: "What are you talking about?"

Gopal: "There was once a hen which laid golden eggs. The owner of the hen felt very lucky that he got the golden eggs and would sell them each day and make a good amount of profit. One day, the farmer's wife asked him that why don't you kill the goose and take out all the gold so that we can become very rich. We both know what the farmer did after that, and we both know he found no gold. The post of the President is a golden eggs laying hen Hari. You can either kill it and try and take all the money at once, or you can let it lay eggs and give you more hens which lay more golden eggs. The bastard Prithvi chose the former. The moment he asked for the money I knew he would do anything to get it. And that included being ridiculed by a junior. Making 13 lacs from this fest will be the biggest mistake he has ever made in life."

Me: "And why is that?"

Gopal: "Because today he lost my respect. And I am going to be the future MP from this area."

Me: "So I guess you will let him have the money. And also, in the story, it was not a hen which laid the golden eggs. It was a goose."

Gopal looked at me, and he smiled. "Hari, as I said, I did not listen to the story. I understood it."

He said this and walked out of the room.

I had never been more proud of my friend.

TWO YEARS LATER

Not much had transpired for me in the two years which had passed. Studies in the University were the usual non-existent but being best friends with a member of the student's council ensured that you did not fail. In fact it ensured that you did pretty well in the exams. These good results would help me when I would go for the civil exams interview.

And yes, I was still cheating on myself by saying that I was studying for the civils. I just had a lot of books on the matter, and would often read history but that was the extent of my devotion to the civil exams.

Nothing at all had happened in my life in the two years that had passed. If anything, I had grown two years older and I cannot take any credit for that. And yes, one more thing had happened, again for which I can take no credit. I was now the best friend of the most powerful man in the University. The plan which Gopal and I had made had been executed flawlessly. In the last two years, Gopal had consolidated his position in the University to such an extent that the party was considering nominating him for the Presidential post even this year. Imagine, a person from the third year becoming the President and fourth year students would be working for him! But he let this pass.

And he was still my best friend.

We both, as usual, were sitting in his room. I had a history book in my hand and he had grandiose dreams of becoming the President. We were both lost in our own worlds, but were still very aware of the presence of each other.

Gopal: "What a journey these last two and a half years have been."

Gopal was in an introspecting mood. He had these fits once in a while.

"And this journey would not have been possible without you. Even if it had been possible, it would have meant nothing."

I just laughed it off.

"No seriously, just imagine from where to where have we come. You remember how shit scared we were when we were taking those pictures of Radha. And look at us today."

I did not understand why he had to bring in Radha into this. Her name did pop into our conversations way more often than it should have.

"So Gopal, where are we headed now?"

"What?"

"Where are we headed now? I mean, there is absolutely no way we can lose the elections next year. You are definitely going to become the President. Not even you can stop that. So what grand plans for this year and the next- our last year in this University."

Gopal: "Remember Hari, around two years back we had a similar conversation. We were wondering what needs to be done in order to ensure that I get a place in the student council in the second year as well. I said that let us organise a fest. You said that the fest would be enough for one year, but we will have to do something new in the coming year. Well, we did not. The fest took us through two years and now here I am. No one can doubt my candidature; no one can doubt my victory next year."

Me: "So another grand fest this year and we are good to go for the next elections?"

Gopal: "Even if we do not do anything, we are good to go for next year my friend. But I do not want to be complacent. I do not want to make the same mistakes the previous Presidents have made. You can see where they all are today. None of them could capitalise on the huge clout we command in the University. You know why that is?"

Me: "Because they killed the hen that laid the golden eggs."

Gopal: "Correct. All of them had a myopic view. And you do not play the game of politics with a myopic view."

Me: "So what's the plan?"

Gopal: "The plan my friend is not to sit back on our past laurels. We have organised the best two fests ever imagined by this University. If we do one more, no one will give a damn. In fact, I am thinking of passing the ownership of the fest to Rohit."

I was kind of surprised, but I was expecting this. "You plan to give away the ace of spades? The fest is our ace of spades Gopal. How can you give it away to a second year student?"

Gopal had a quiet laugh. "If I say I see myself in him, will that be a good enough reason?"

I smiled back at him. The question was not who he was giving it to, the question was why.

"Hari, we have to do something else this year. Something, which like the fest, has not even been thought of by anyone so far in the history of our University."

Me: "And what is that?"

Gopal: "As you had said two years ago, let's sleep over it."

Me: "And please, this time don't wake me up in the middle of the night to tell me the plan. I guess we can both wait till the sun rises."

Gopal and I, both smiled and both took our beds. This was the only air conditioned room in the hostel. Not even the current President had one.

And this time, Gopal did not wake me in the middle of the night.

This time, I did.

Gopal was awakened by a glass of cold water on his head. Surprisingly, he was pretty normal when he woke up. No bad mouthing, no irritation, in fact a little smile on his face.

Me: "Why aren't you irritated or shouting? I just emptied a glass of cold water over your head!"

Gopal: "I had a premonition, that this time it would not be me waking you up but vice versa. And guess what, I was right. So tell me, what is it?"

Me: "I have found my iPod."

Gopal: "What? I am going to kill you. Don't tell me that you woke me in the middle of the night to tell me that you have found your lost iPod. I am really going to hit you now!"

I smiled at the innocence of my friend. The only thought in his life was politics.

Me: "No you idiot. I have not found my lost iPod. I have found *my iPod*. Like Steve Jobs made an iPod and changed his company, I have found my iPod."

Gopal looked at his watch. "Hari, it is 4 am. If you do not stop these riddles and tell me what is in your mind, I swear to God that I will find your iPod and do things with it to you which you will not like."

Now these were the kind of reactions I was expecting when I woke him at 4 am.

Me: "Ok, ok. I will tell you what will make us immortal. Women." Gopal looked at me. And waited. And finally spoke "Please go on."

Me: "In our college, girls have absolutely no say. They cannot walk in peace, they cannot talk in peace, and due to some bad people like us, they sometimes only *rest in peace.*"

I know what I had said was not funny. Gopal did not even consider it worth a comment. So after a brief pause, I changed my tone to a more serious nature and continued.

"So, as I was saying. Girls have absolutely no role to play in our college. They are eve teased openly. They do not have proper hostels to live, they cannot take part in any college activities, and God forbid, if they are seen with any guy, they are branded sluts for the rest of their lives."

Gopal: "So what are you saying?"

Me: "I am saying, let's use them. We have used a girl before to our advantage and we can both see how that has worked out for us. Remember, the first year membership in the council, the funds for the two grand fests, all have been possible only because of a girl."

I gave a brief pause. I let the thought sink in. Gopal was completely out of his slumber now. He was listening to every word I was saying, and he was thinking.

Gopal: "So what is your plan?"

Me: "My plan is that we reach out to the girls of our University. If anyone can even think of giving them equal status, it is you. No one can dare do anything against what you want. So if we give girls an equal status, we have them all on our side. And, from next year, there is a compulsory 35% reservation for girl students in the University. That will give them a sizeable number.

Even in history, women have always played a very important part in politics. When we were out to get to Radha, you used the example of Draupadi. But women have not only led to wars and victories, they have also been leaders in wars. Be it Cleopatra who took away all the power from her husband and brother Ptolemy, or be it Rani Lakshmi Bai who ruled Jhansi alone and took the powerful Britishers head on or be it Razia Sultan , who at that time refused to be called the female version of the word Sultan which was Sultana and meant 'wife or a mistress of a Sultan' and hence called herself Razia Sultan and not Razia Sultana."

Gopal was still in deep thought. "Brilliant. This is simply brilliant. This is a hundred times better than the fest. And as you said, this is *your* iPod. I want you to lead this."

I could not believe what he had said. We had been friends for a very long time now but this was the first time he had actually given me a political responsibility.

"Let's start working on this from today itself. You are right. This is going to change everything. Hari my boy, you have given me a new dream. In the elections next year, I want to win by the greatest margin ever recorded in the history of our University."

Gopal said this and went back to slumber. The plan was made. Girls were to be our next target. How, when, and where was to be decided by me. I would now have many sleepless nights in front of me. I had to make this work if I wanted to create an identity for myself. I had to make *my iPod* work.

I started off with a recce of the girl's hostel and the conditions in which they lived. Being a friend of Gopal, getting permission to enter the hostel was a non issue.

I entered the hostel, and it looked pretty much like the boys hostel. The ratio of girls to boys in our hostel at present was about one is to ten and so there was this only one small hostel for all girls. I was the only male inside and I too carried a letter signed by Gopal himself. Even the guard was a lady.

"Who do you want to meet?"

"How does it matter to you?"

Being with Gopal had taught me how to deal with people who we considered unimportant. I showed her the letter, she let me in.

I entered through one corridor which led to the mess. It was 11 am and I did not see anyone in the mess. I entered pretty confidently and that is when I saw her, and that is when my entire life, and the life of a lot of people around me, changed.

She was running after one of her friends, and both of them were giggling in a way only girls can. The other girl, Sohna her name was, as I would later get to know, had her dupatta in her hand and was running away to glory. She did not see me, least of all expect me, and ran straight into my arms and I held her, but my eyes never left her eyes. Never left the eyes of my Radha.

Sohna was in my arms and was about to fall. She hung on looking at me, but my eyes refused to budge. The were looking straight ahead. They were staring into two specs of the whole universe, they were looking into the blue of the sea and green of the land, they were looking into the deep abyss of infinity. My eyes were looking into their own future, they were looking into Radha's eyes.

And after what seemed an eternity, but was actually just a couple of seconds, the grip of my arms around Sohna loosened and she fell onto the ground with a loud thud and a scream.

"Radha, help me."

Radha took her eyes away from me but instead of concern for her friend, I could see a longing to extend the moments we had lived. Something which she would have seen in my eyes as well.

Sohna got up herself, gave me an angry look, took Radha's hand, and they left, Sohna grumbling as she was leaving "I don't know who gives such people admission into the girl's hostel. If they want votes, why don't they go to the boy's hostel? Why do they have to come here? Losers....."

The grumbling continued and my eyes kept following her hoping that she would turn back. The girl is always supposed to turn back, that is what we have read in books, that is what we have seen in movies. The girl always turns back.

But she was quietly ushered into a room. And I stood there waiting. And waiting.

And she did not come back.

The recce of the hostel was now done half heartedly. I could not get my mind off her. In the evening I was sitting with Gopal and he asked me how it had been. I started mumbling, and he, as only best friends can, got to know that there was something else which was occupying my head.

"What happened? Did mother send another letter from the village? Do you need more money? How many times have I told you that you just need to ask. We still have a large portion of the gold which Radha had left. And I have told you so many times that that money is as much yours as is mine."

"No Gopal, mother is fine. In fact, the last time we had sent her money, she had actually started a small tailoring shop and it is now doing pretty well."

"Then what is the issue? I have never seen you so offbeat?"

I smiled. "I saw her today. I saw Radha."

The color went off Gopal's face. I then realised what I had said would have sounded.

"No, no, no, no. Not that Radha. I saw my Radha."

Gopal was somewhat relieved, but curious. "What? Don't spin tales. Tell me what happened."

And then I told him. Told him how I had fallen in love.

Gopal fell on the ground laughing when the name Radha came up again. We called in a first year student into our room, Rohan, and within half an hour had all information we needed about her.

Rohan (very nervously), "Sir, her name is Radha Malik. She is from a small town, Joginder Nagar, in Himachal Pradesh and is in the first year. Her father is a small businessman and has reluctantly allowed his only daughter to come all the way for studies. She is an only child and her mother had passed away when she was 5."

Gopal, "When her mother was five?"

Rohan (even more nervously) "No sir, when Radha was five."

Gopal, "Talk properly you idiot."

Gopal used to get kicks in making other people uncomfortable. Rohan now started again, almost bathing in sweat.

"She is a very pretty, bubbly and lively girl and everyone in the girl's hostel has taken an instant liking towards her. She is a very good badminton player and wants to organise a tournament in the girl's hostel as the one which we did in our fests did not allow participation from the girls."

Gopal- "You like her?"

Rohan- "Sorry sir."

Gopal, with a smile on his face "What did I ask you?"

Rohan- "Sorry sir."

Gopal- "Again the same thing. What did I ask you idiot?"

Rohan- "You asked me if I liked her."

Gopal- "Very good. Now tell me, do you like her?"

Rohan- "No sir."

Gopal- "You don't like pretty girls?"

Rohan- "Sorry sir."

Gopal- "Again sorry."

This could have continued forever so I intervened and asked Rohan to run off.

Gopal- "This, this is the future of our hostel. Good thing you thought of getting girls on our side. You think idiots like this Rohan will win us elections in three years? Idiot."

Me: "Let it go. So tell me, what do you think?"

Gopal "I think it's brilliant. Did you hear the last part? The girl wants to organise a tournament. How many girls in our college can even think like that? Get hold of that girl. She will be of great help to us."

I had actually asked him about my love life but the conversation had veered in a completely different direction.

"But how will a girl in the first year help us?"

"My dear Hari. How many girls are there in our college right now?"

He did not wait for an answer.

"With the 35% reservation for girls next year, the number of girls in the first year will be more than the total number of girls right now. And who will girls in first year listen to?"

He again did not wait for an answer.

"They will listen to girls in the second year."

I intervened. "Remember, when we were in the first year, all the first year students followed only Prithvi, who was in the fourth year."

"That is correct. But that is because he was a leader. We are not going to comment on what sort of leader, but people followed him, looked up to him. Next year, will a first year girl have anyone to look up to?"

He continued. "No, she will not. When it comes to politics, the fourth year ones will ask them to stay away from the dirty game and the dirty boys who play this game. This is because that is what they would have seen throughout their years in college. But, if we, in fact, if you do something and make this Radha girl popular, she will dictate terms in the next elections."

The plan made sense. The third and fourth year ones were too old into the system to change. We had to influence the first year ones. Plus, next year, they would have maximum interaction with the new freshers and it was mainly the freshers who we were targeting.

"And also Hari. Radha has always helped us in the elections."

He winked at me as he said this and got down into reading some magazine. I don't know why, but the name of Radha kept creeping in our conversations from time to time. I did not know whether he was guilty of what he did, or whether he was proud. In fact, even I was not sure what I felt. I was as much responsible for what had happened as Gopal was. I was definitely not proud. But I did not feel guilty either. It was something which I had done for a friend and if asked again, I would do it again. It was as simple as that.

The next day, I lined up in front of the first year lecture halls. There was an exam that day so the halls were full. As time got over, the students left the hall. All of them bowing their heads, or showing some sort of respect for me.

And then there she was. Standing ten feet away from me, and I could again not look away from her eyes. The same eyes.

The whole crowd passed, a little more quickly than usual because I was standing there, and we kept on staring. When the area was almost empty, she raised her eyebrows once, in question.

I smiled, and raised mine.

She raised them twice, and I did the same.

It did take some guts from her side to do such a thing with a senior. And that too me, Gopal's friend.

I walked up to her.

"We can keep on doing this forever."

"It's the guy's onus to come and talk."

She had guts, to talk to me like that.

"So here I am."

"So what do I do?"

More guts.

"You tell me why you did not look back the other day."

"Because if I did, we might not have been having this conversation."

She said this and looked down, blushing. She was the girl after all. I continued.

"Do you know me?"

"Who doesn't know you? You are Gopal sir's friend."

"Hari."

"Radha."

The name felt even sweeter coming from her mouth.

"I have to leave. If someone sees us...."

I gave a little laugh. A laugh filled with power.

"You are standing with me. Hari. No one will dare."

"I know that. It's just that people will talk."

"So where do we meet?"

"The same place where we met the first time?"

"The girl's hostel?"

She nodded.

"I don't have permission to come in their every day."

"You are *Hari*. I am sure you will find a way."

She smiled and left. My hands were on my head and I was unsure whether she was mocking me or praising me. Whatever she was doing, it felt nice. It had never felt this nice before.

I told Gopal what happened. He smiled and went looking into his cupboard. He took out an old note book, tore out a page and gave it to me.

"What is this?"

"The poem I wrote for Radha when we had met for the first time. Had worked like magic on her. I bet it will work on this Radha as well."

And then as an afterthought. "Don't worry about entry into the hostel. You just concentrate on her. I like her attitude and the way she thinks. She can definitely help us. In this time, we do need some girls on our side."

I, in the meanwhile, was lost in my thoughts. I read the poem which Gopal had written and I did not know that there was such a romantic heart under that political head. I wanted to make an impression, I wanted to do something out of this world for her, I wanted Radha to fall for me- and not only for political reasons. This was the first time I had been attracted to a girl in such a manner. Of course there used to be the girls at the victory parties of elections and otherwise in the city as well, but this feeling was not physical. This went way beyond that. It felt different, it felt crazy. It felt like love.

Radha had dared me, so initially I thought I would make a daring entry into her hostel. I thought I would enter during dinner time at the mess, and in front of everyone would sweep her in my arms and take her with me. But then thought it would be too outlandish, so I chose a more romantic way.

This time I made an entry from the back side of the hostel. Rohan, the first year junior, had helped me with her room number and location. I entered her balcony, and there she was. Sitting. Reading. She was the most beautiful girl I had ever seen in my life. I wondered if the reading part was a facade and if she was thinking of me the way I had been thinking of her ever since I had seen her.

I had planned to make this romantic but just looking at her then gave me such an uncontrollable urge that I could not stop myself and was about to open the balcony door when suddenly her main door opened.

Sohna, " Radha, let's go."

Radha was completely lost in her thoughts.

Sohna (in a louder voice), "Radha!"

Radha, "Oh sorry, I just didn't notice you."

Sohna, "Yeah, yeah, why will you notice me now? Now you will only notice one person."

I did not know who they were talking about. If it was anyone but me, I swore I would kill him.

Radha (innocently), "Who? What are you talking about?"

Sohna, "Now come on. You can play that innocent Radha in front of someone else. Everyone saw you talking to that good looking guy in the afternoon."

I blushed. I think for the first time in my life. Girls actually thought I was good looking.

Radha, "Who? Hari?"

Sohna, "I don't know his name. But Gopal's friend."

Radha, "Yes, he has a name. It's Hari. And no, we hardly know each other."

Sohna, "Hmm. So do you want to know him better?"

Radha did not say anything but just smiled and hit her friend with a pillow.

Radha, "Such stuff is all you can talk about."

Sohna, "It will be brilliant. When you two get hooked up, why don't you fix me up with Gopal."

And then in a dramatic tone. "Just imagine. Next year, I will be the first lady of the college."

Radha, "First lady?"

Sohna, "President's girlfriend you idiot."

She said this and both started giggling.

Radha, "Here that idiot Hari has not even approached me yet. And you start dreaming of your love life."

They both kept giggling and moved out of the room. For dinner I guess.

The blush on my face had given way to the biggest smile ever seen on any man's face. The battle had already been won. I now had to ensure that I did not spoil it.

I entered the room through the balcony and carried my bag with me.

Radha entered the room 20 minutes later, this time thankfully without Sohna. That was enough time for me to do what I had planned.

It was dead dark when she entered. She closed the door behind her looking for the light. I took out a matchstick and put it next to my face. Surprisingly, she was not scared. I guess, on some level she had expected me. I lit one candle and the connections which I had made in the last twenty minutes made the word 'RADHA' light up in her room. With small candles.

The surprise on her face changed to a smile and then I pressed a switch and a flashlight came on above her head, making a halo over her in the otherwise dark room. She could now see me. I had a guitar in my hand and I started. Frank Sinatra.

Some day, when I'm awfully low,
When the world is cold,
I will feel a glow just thinking of you
And the way you look tonight.

She settled on her bed and had a warm smile on her face. Listening, and waiting for more.

Yes you're lovely, with your smile so warm
And your cheeks so soft,
There is nothing for me but to love you,
And the way you look tonight

To me it appeared as if the song was written for me and for this very moment. She blushed and looked down. And then looked up again. Again listening, and again waiting for more.

With each word your tenderness grows,
Tearing my fear apart
And that laugh that wrinkles your nose,
It touches my foolish heart.

The song had now stopped making sense in the moment. But she was still mesmerised, and I continued and finished the song

Lovely, never, ever change.

Keep that breathless charm.

Won't you please arrange it ?

Cause I love you, just the way you look tonight.

And then just to round it off.

Just the way you look to-night.

She got up, her eyes still mesmerised by what I had done for her, and with a seductive tone to her walk, she came over to me.

She removed the guitar from the sling around my shoulders. Never had I let go of control in such a manner. Never had I felt what I was feeling now. Never had I thought that this would be possible.

We looked into each other's eyes. The eyes which I had seen for the first time only sometime ago. The eyes which were two specs of the whole universe, which were the blue of the sea and green of the land, which were the deep abyss of infinity, in which I could see my own future. The eyes which meant the whole world to me.

And we kissed. The first kiss. A long first kiss.

And then we looked into each other again. Nothing had been spoken for the last five minutes. I finally opened my mouth.

"I love you." Yes. It was the truth. I was madly in love with her.

She smiled. A playful one. And then went back and sat on her bed.

"Anyone can use a Frank Sinatra song and impress a girl. Show me something original."

I smiled back. Initially I had rehearsed the poem which Gopal had given me and had made a junior come up with some sort of tune for it on the guitar. I had learnt that but at the last moment had found Frank Sinatra more impressive. But Gopal's poem was also going to be used.

So I started again, with full sincerity.

It's not because of the woods
It's not because of the sky
It's not because of the little leaves floating in your chai

It's not because of the light
It's not because of the dark
It's not because of the butterflies flying in the park

It's not because of the wind
It's not because of the glow
It's not because of the raindrops falling with the snow

It's not because of the colours
Red, Green and Blue
The reason that the world is beautiful

Is You, you.. You!

And this time, there was no smile, no surprise. This time, there were tears in her eyes. And I knew I had her. Forever.

Our love affair continued, and blossomed as the days went by. I grew addicted to her. She was one of those who wanted to attend classes and actually study engineering, so I used to accompany her to lectures every day. We would then go and have lunch together, take small walks and say sweet nothings into each other's ears. When not with each other, we would continue the sweet nothings over SMS, and in the night, I would visit her at least once to say goodnight. It was like a fairytale for me. I was from a small village and never had I even heard of such kind of affection. I was in a world of my own, a world in which only Radha and I existed, unassuming to all around us. And this is how I wanted this world to be.

Also, this was the first high profile affair our University had seen. Never before had a first year girl been so openly in love. One day, I was having lunch in the canteen with Radha and her friends and one of her friends broached the subject.

Geeta, "You know Hari. Even I have a boyfriend now. He is in the first year. His name is Rohan. He is also from your hostel."

A smile appeared on my face. This was the same Rohan who had almost peed in his pants in front of me and Gopal when we had asked him information about Radha.

"That is very nice."

Geeta, "What nice? I can't even talk to him in public. He is only a mobile phone boyfriend. He says that if any senior sees him talking to a girl, he will be thrashed to death. Please don't tell anyone. He is in your hostel only, right?"

I nodded, the smile still fixed on my face. I enjoyed the power which I had. I looked at Radha with a proud smile on my face. She could be with me anytime she wanted.

Geeta, "I wish he was also friends with Gopal. Then we could also have walks, we could also eat food in the canteen," then with a twinkle in her eye "we could also spend the nights together."

The girls started giggling and the same smile continued on my face. I was used to such banter but Radha would get very embarrassed and would turn tomato red. I looked at her face, and it was red. But this was not the red because of embarrassment, this was a different red. This was a red of anger. The red I had seen a few times in the past to know its consequences.

The normal chit chat continued for some time but the color on Radha's face did not change. And she did not participate in the conversation anymore. After some awkward moments, where questions asked to Radha went unanswered, we got up and moved on towards the girl's hostel. The other girl's had to go to the library and asked Radha if she would accompany them. A horizontal movement of the head told them she did not want to go and Radha and I headed towards her hostel.

Me, "What's wrong baby?"

Words like baby, coochie, darling, honey etc were now part of almost all my conversations. And I knew the answer before she would say anything. I knew she would say "nothing is wrong." I would have to dig deeper.

Radha, "Something is seriously wrong."

This was really serious. She admitted something was wrong in the first go.

"What happened honey?"

Radha,"I don't like this."

Me, "Don't like what?" And then just to be a little cute and dampen her anger, "You don't like me calling you honey? Okay, I will call you darling. How does that sound?"

She paid no heed at my attempt at cheesiness.

Radha, "I don't like the way people treat you."

She said this and a tear trickled down her face. And before I could say or do anything, there was a whole array of tears. Radha was a very strong girl. This was the first time she had cried in front of me. I moved in front of her and hugged her and looked into her eyes. The tears still did not stop. I hugged her, and she planted her face on my chest and continued the crying. We could do such things in the University. I was after all Gopal's best friend.

And then she started to sob.

Me, "What happened, my dear? Did anyone say anything to you? You tell me. You know I can take care of it."

Radha, still crying, but managing to speak, "No. No one can say anything to me in this University. After all, I am the girl friend of Gopal's best friend."

I almost put a smile on my face as she acknowledged my position in the University but then the sobs turned into a howl. And then she stopped. She moved back from my shoulder and she continued.

"How long will I be the girl friend of Gopal's best friend? What has he done for the hostel and for his party what you haven't? I have asked everyone and all of them told me that both of you have slogged your asses over the past three years to make him what he is today."

She paused. I did not know what to say. These were lines on which I had never even thought of thinking.

"Both of you slog your asses, but what happens after three years? My friends say that I can talk to you in public because you are Gopal's friend. Not because you yourself are Hari, but because you are Gopal's friend. What happened when I told Sohna that I liked you? She said that you hook up with Gopal's best friend, and then help me hook up with Gopal so that I can become the first lady of the campus. What the fuck? She did not even know your name Hari. No one knows you for who you are. People just know you for being Gopal's best friend. Gopal, Gopal, Gopal, Gopal, Gopal. This is all I hear. Both of you work hard, both of you care only about your hostel, but it is only Gopal who walks away with all the credit. Tell me, had Gopal not been there, would you have the guts to hug me in the centre of the road? Tell me."

I did not know what to say.

"Tell me. See, you don't have an answer. Nobody knows who you are Hari, and nobody cares and hence nobody has said this to you before. But I care, Hari. I care for you."

She said this and hugged me and the tears started flowing again.

"I love you more than anything in this world, Hari. And I cannot see you being humiliated every day. Has Gopal ever made you the hero? Has he ever given you the credit? Has he ever given you the responsibility? In all these years has he ever even thought of including *you* in the student's council?"

As she cried on my shoulder, I thought of answers to these questions for the first time in my life.

And for the first time, I felt cheated.

Because the answer to all these questions was a no. No, he had never made me the hero, no he had never given me the credit, no, he had never given me any responsibility except the one with respect to Radha because he knew he could not do it alone, and no, even after a couple of hints, he had not even thought of including me in the council. And then she asked me the biggest question.

Radha, "Leave the post of the President, is he going to nominate you for any post in the next year's election?"

I thought of it and the only answer I could think of was no. No, he would not nominate me for any post. He would make me work for the party, he would make me get all the girls support through Radha, but he would never nominate me for any post in the party.

A tear trickled down my cheek as well. I moved Radha from my chest and I left. She stood there crying and calling out my name, but I had more important answers to look out for. As I walked from her hostel to mine, myriad thoughts came to my mind. I did not know why I could not see all this earlier, I could not understand why Gopal was doing this to me, I could not understand where had I gone wrong in our friendship. I wondered if he even thought this was a friendship. Did he think of himself as the guru and of me as the disciple? Was that my position after all those years of trust and hard work?

Tears were now freely flowing down my cheeks and as I crossed the small market, a shopkeeper on seeing me said, "Baba, say hello to Gopal sir."

And I lost it.

I charged inside the shop and picked up the steel bowl in which he kept the paan leaves and hit him on his head with it. And I kept hitting him until the whole market surrounded me and had to stop me. And I kept on saying one thing "Why the fuck are you not saying hello to me?"

After the crowd took control of me, and took the paan wala to the hospital, I continued my journey to the hostel. I walked into Gopal's room and he was chatting to some other hostel members. A smile appeared on his face when he saw me. He spoke.

Gopal, "Such auspicious timing my friend. Such auspicious timing." He then saw my torn shirt and with a look of concern- "What happened, Hari? All fine?"

Me, "Yes, had a minor altercation in the market."

Gopal, "I hope nothing serious, should I send someone?"

Me, "No Gopal, I am fine. I can take care of myself."

A smile appeared on Gopal's face. A smile which on any other day I would have thought was of content. But today it seemed like contempt.

Gopal, "Yes, so the auspicious moment. We have just finalised the list of contenders for next year's elections. And how could I make this public without you?"

My heart started beating the way it had when I had first made love. I wanted to see the names on that list. And more than anything in this world, I wanted my name to be on it, for our friendship's sake, for Gopal's sake, for my sake.

Gopal, "President- Gopal Kashyap."

3 names to go.

"Treasurer- Puneet Singh."

2 names to go.

"General secretary- Vikram Varshney."

The last name.

"Cultural secretary- Prashant Panwar."

And that was it. That was the end of our friendship, a friendship which I was not even sure had ever existed. That was the end of Gopal and me.

Gopal hugged me as he completed reading out the names. "You wait and watch, Hari. After you get all the girls on our side, next year would be the biggest victory in the history of our hostel."

Me, "Yes, Gopal. I will wait and watch." And then to myself- "As I have for the last three years. Waited and watched."

Gopal moved out of the room along with the others to announce the nominations, leaving me behind. And I again could not hold on. And I cried. I cried to a lost friend, I cried to a wasted three years, I cried to myself.

The next few days were spent all alone in my room. I did not even talk to Radha and I think even she understood why. The fifth day, since I had completely given up on the outside world, a very concerned Gopal walked into my room.

Gopal, "What happened, Hari? I have been a little busy after announcing the nominations. You know the usual ego pleasing of the people who have missed out. I just missed out on having you around. Someone told me that something is wrong. What happened? You know you can tell me everything. You know I can take care of everything."

I was on my bed with my back facing Gopal. A fit of anger engulfed me after the last sentence. *You know I can take care of everything.* It was me who was responsible for the power he was talking about. It was me. And he again took all the credit. All to himself. *You know I can take care of everything.* That asshole of a man, that asshole of a friend.

I just stay put, the anger had to be used in a better and more constructive way. I shut my eyes tight, a few droplets fell down.

Gopal, "What happened, Hari? Are you asleep? Hari, Hari."

He shook me to check if I was sleeping. I played along and in a very sleepy voice murmured.

"Who is it?"

Gopal, with a lot of concern on hearing my forlorn voice, "Hari it is me, Gopal. Tell me what happened, my friend. I will take care of everything. You know I can take care of everything."

Those lines again. *You know I can take care of everything.*

Gopal, "Hari."

I had to speak up. I did not know what to say, but before I could speak, Gopal gave me the answer.

Gopal, "Is it Radha?"

Me, "Hi, Gopal. Sorry I could not help in the last few days. Yes, it is Radha. Friendship makes you so miserable."

Gopal, "Not friendship my friend, love. It is love which makes you miserable. Friendship only gives you strength."

He could very well say that. All his strength was because of me.

Gopal, "Look here brother."

And I turned.

He saw me. And smiled. In a different time I would have thought this was a smile of concern. But I now knew it was contempt. Contempt for a disciple who could not take care of himself.

Gopal, "Does this Radha also deserve what we had done to the previous one?"

There was a smirk in his eye. I could still not figure out whether there was any hint of guilt.

I faked a smile.

Gopal, "Tell me. What did she do?"

Me, "Nothing. You know, the usual girl stuff. I think it's the wrong month of the year."

Gopal, "Wrong month of the year?"

Hari, "I mean wrong day of the month."

Gopal, "You need my help? You know I can do anything to help you."

Hari, "No thank you. I think I have this covered. Just need some time alone. I will get over it and back with her."

Gopal smiled again. "Should I leave?"

Hari, "Yes, I need some time. In fact, I think I will call her and talk to her to settle things."

Gopal, "Anything for you brother. Anything for you."

Gopal got up and before leaving the room asked, "So what do you think?"

Me, "About what?"

Gopal, "About whether she will be ready to help us in the elections next year."

Me, "I think she already is. All her year girls like her. With the kind of personality she has and the kind of platform we can provide, I don't foresee any problems for next year."

Gopal smiled. "Good." The smile then vanished. "Hari, all this love nonsense is fine, but I hope you remember the ultimate goal. We have to use this girl for our benefit. She has to help us in the next elections."

I nodded and he left. My master had delivered his sermon and had told me how to conduct myself *even* in my love life. Had he stayed for even a minute longer, I swear, I would have killed him.

The days kept on passing, but the anger within me refused to cease. I tried to keep myself distant from Gopal and though he showed some concern in the beginning, he gradually got too busy in the build up to the elections. But whenever we would meet, he would definitely ask about Radha and at most times would slip in the sermon of remembering the final goal. I, who till now had been an important part of his election campaign, was reduced to a mere bystander and he did not seem to care.

In the meanwhile, I grew closer to Radha. After the showdown in which she had made me realise how unfair Gopal had been on me, we had only had that conversation one more time, a month after the first one, when she asked me how I felt on not being nominated for any post and being completely sidelined. And I did not hold back. I told her exactly how I felt. How I wanted to kill Gopal.

She did not broach the subject after that. I think she understood that it was a wound which would be fresh for a very very long time. And I had not been able to decide what would I do or how I would avenge the humiliation. And I think she thought that I was too powerless to do anything. So we both did not talk about it and the topic died a natural death.

And the days kept on passing, and I had nothing but more anger, more grief and more humiliation to show for it.

It was now time for the annual college fest. Gopal was now obviously caught up in more important work and the lowly work of organising it had come upon me. But the master had delivered a sermon. He had asked me to include Radha in the organising committee of the fest as next year, if she spoke to the fresher girls as the first female member of the organising committee, it would carry a hell lot of weight. I agreed to what my master had to say and Radha was included in the committee.

The fest was brilliant again, now we did not even have to dig into our coffers of gold for the money. The success of the previous year's fests had ensured that sponsors took good care of all the expenses. At one moment I thought that I would take away all the money which was hidden in the form of gold, and take Radha, and run away. But I knew better. First, both of us, Gopal and I had separate keys which had to be used in unison to get to the gold. I knew I could somehow manage that and get the gold. But I knew Gopal did not care for money. If I took the money, it would not affect him the least. Power is what he wanted. So I decided against it and continued my mundane job of getting the fest together.

Radha participated very actively during the entire duration of organising and execution and Gopal, as usual, was right. Radha had earned a sort of respect which was unheard of for women in this part of the country.

Radha, in her new role, had also joined our party. Again, the first girl to do so. And she had even started interacting with Gopal on important matters.

And I was seen by Gopal as the man who had set the girl's angle right for him. The person he could always turn to when needed, but who did not want anything in return. The perfect fool he had had with him for the last three years who had made him what he was.

I did not share my feelings towards Gopal with anyone. Not even Radha. In fact I think she even got over the fact that she had ignited such a fire within me and when in front of her, even I acted aloof and above all this. I even lied to her that I had no political ambitions and all that I had told her earlier when I was not nominated for any post, was all spur of the moment and I had not meant a single word of it. I reminded her about my civil exams aspirations and in lieu of that, I would spend endless days in my room, alone, staring at the walls, looking into nothing, and thinking about nothing at all. I could not get to make up my mind how I would get back at Gopal. As the days passed by, the thoughts turned to whether I *could* get back at Gopal.

With my permanent absence, and the political ambitions of Radha, she grew close to Gopal. The relationship was absolutely platonic, in fact, he considered her a younger sister. He would never let any harm come to his *best friend's* love, or at least that is what he said.

Radha gradually forgot what she had said about Gopal and me. She had accepted the fact that I was nobody and was ok with it. I am not sure whether she was ok with it or had decided to live with it but she did not let it be a cause of concern in our relationship anymore.

THE FINAL YEAR

The final year had now started. The journey which we had started three years ago was to culminate in this year which would govern where our future took us. The condition of the economy had improved and some companies had even taken the pain of visiting our campus to interview for jobs. Few of us would get jobs, and Gopal, being the great man and master he was, had assured me a job from campus if I did not make it through to the civils. For me, the civils had become a joke but some of us, who had stayed away from politics and fests and girls would actually make it. Some would go for further studies, MBA or M Tech maybe, while the others would just go away, back to the small villages and towns they had come from and would start life afresh. A life with a degree that did not matter, and an education that did not happen.

Gopal on the other hand would join mainstream politics and no one would be surprised if in ten years he would become the MLA or even the MP from the area. Such was the importance and respect he already commanded, even within the senior non University wing of the party. His master plan, in fact my master plan, of getting girls on our side had worked brilliantly and all the new girls were already singing to the tune of Radha.

And Radha was singing to the tune of Gopal. Even she had political ambitions in her head and she knew that Gopal was the one who would get her there. She knew that no one was ready for a girl in the student's council this year, or maybe even the next, but by the time she got to the fourth year, the President's post was what she was eyeing. She knew that one simple smile would get her all the men votes, and she already had a huge clout among the women.

She told me of her plans and dreams on and off whenever we talked. The frequency and duration of our conversations had greatly reduced since the time we had started dating. And maybe even the love. Initially it was because I had gone into a shell (and had blamed it on the civil exams), and then because honestly, she was busier than me. Gopal trusted her almost as much as he trusted me and the work which used to be mine earlier, due to my civil exam studies, had been transferred to her. He treated her like a younger sister and she thoroughly enjoyed the treatment. She reminded me of a Gopal when he was in that position and at that age. I was just not sure how far she could go to get the President seat. Could she go as far as Gopal and I had gone?

The respect which I commanded when I walked in the market, when I roamed the lecture halls had subsided to a great degree and everyday killed me a little by little. The every *salaam* missed, the every bow of the head missed by a junior, everything just killed me.

And there was nothing I could do about it. I had made Gopal, and now I had made Radha. And I was alone.

And then one day, a day before the elections, the inevitable happened.

I was walking around the market, with absolutely no interest in the elections or anything related to it, and obviously lonely because Radha was hell busy with the kind of duties I used to do before the elections, and Gopal because he had a dream of making this the biggest victory ever, when a group of first year students walked passed by me. They saw me and said.

"Sir. You are Radha's boyfriend right. Please wish her good luck for the elections tomorrow."

From being *Gopal's best friend*, I was now *Radha's boyfriend*.

Unimportant, unwanted, inconsequential, insignificant.

I did not hit those students because I knew it would not help. There was something which was brewing in my head which I had been unsure of over the last few months. It was now time to execute it. It was all or nothing.

GOPAL'S STORY

It was the same day, a day before the elections. This time, I was the party leader and was contesting for the President. What Prithvi had said three years ago had come true to the last bit. Gandhi Bhavan had now been reduced to nothing. Radha and Surya, and the guilt of their deaths had long gone, and Radha's father was still in prison, for the double murder. There was a new Radha in my life now, a Radha who was the love of my best friend and most trusted aide- Hari, and this Radha would help me make history. This Radha would make me win the election by a record margin by getting all the girl votes for me.

I sat in my room, satisfied on how I had planned and lived through the last three years. From having a hand in two murders, to making a friend who would die for me, to being the first first year student in the students council, to being the Presidential candidate and in a day from now, creating history by winning by the greatest margin ever. If God had written this story, he could not have scripted it better than this.

Also, looking at our complete domination, the stakes in college politics had been raised manifold. The President now got direct entry into the senior party and would be an active member involved in the decisions that affected the centre.

Being the President of our college was now a sure shot way of getting into the big league. And I was right on track.

I was sitting with Hari in my room and he was, as usual, talking about history. We had not been together that often lately. Hari was too busy studying for his civils, and whatever free time he got he liked to spend it with Radha. After a long time he had come to my room to just sit and chat. I was in a self extolling mode I wanted to talk about how big a margin I would win the next day. I would predict the biggest margin ever, but Hari wanted to talk about something else as I guess he would have been hearing the same thing day in and day out from Radha. So I let him.

Our friendship had grown over the years to something which went much beyond trust and understanding, and now, even communicating. Unlike earlier, now we would go days without speaking to each other but when we used to meet, and sit like this, everything used to be the same. I thought of the day we had met for the first time, the run through the streets of the town, running away from the Gandhi Bhavan seniors. How life had changed from that day to this. How we had grown from that day to this, how our love had grown, how our bond had grown.

How could one friend mean so much, how he could complete every aspect of my life. If I was the king, he was the perfect minister, always knowing the right thing to say, the right thing to do. I wondered at times, what would I be without him.

Hari had a very particular story to tell me that day. It had been a very long time since I had last listened to one of his history stories. They were always interesting and always had a message to be shared, understood and implemented. He started off.

"Remember, when we were sitting in our first year room, waiting for time to pass so that we could go and click the pictures of Radha, I said some lines to you which you did not understand."

The name of the *earlier* Radha continued to be a constant in our conversations. Even the mention of her name would earlier give me fits. But I was over that now. I could talk about her with the same indifference that I would talk about the chicken I ate last night.

"If I did not understand it then, how do you expect me to understand it now?"

He smiled, like he always did. A smile which spelt warmth, which spelt love.

"I will repeat

> Between the acting of a dreadful thing
> And the first motion, all the interim is
> Like a phantasma, or a hideous dream"

"What is that?" I said. Still, as clueless as I was when the first time I had heard this.

"Having decided that Caesar must die, Brutus reflects on how difficult it is to put his decision into action," replied Hari.

"What?" I said again.

"Last time when I said these lines, we had the exact same conversation. And you asked me what it meant, and I told you the time would come when I will tell you this story."

"What story?"

"The story of Julius Caeser and his trusted aide and friend, Brutus."

He continued.

"Julius Caeser had declared himself as 'dictator for life' of the Roman empire and had included Brutus in his inner circle. In fact, he made Brutus the governor of one of his estates when he had gone to Africa for further conquests. But the senators were growing wary, and jealous, of the power that Julius Caeser had bestowed upon himself. Almost all the important decisions were taken by Caeser. Brutus, or any other member of the senate, would think of a brilliant plan and would implement it but guess who would walk away with all the credit and glory?"

Me, "Julius Caeser."

"Correct. And the most affected of all of Caeser's misgivings was of course Brutus. Brutus just came to be known as the trusted aide of Caeser wherein all the effort into making what Caeser had become had been done by him. In fact, it was not only Brutus who felt cheated, he was the last one to actually realise what had been done to him. It was the senate which felt undone and all of them contrived to kill Caeser.

All of them, including Brutus.

When Caeser was finally attacked by the senators in his own senate, he dealt with one blow after the other but when he saw that his trusted Brutus was also among those who intended to kill him, he could take it no more. The last words he said before he died were "Et tu, Brute?" which means "You too Brutus?""

There was a certain uneasiness in the way Hari was telling this story to me. A certain uneasiness which I had never before felt in our friendship.

"Hari, why are you telling this to me?"

"The story is not over yet. When Caeser was killed, the Roman crowd wanted to know why Brutus had done what he had. Why he had killed his own friend who had loved him more than his own life. Brutus replied- "Not that I loved Caeser less, but that I loved Rome more.""

I had a confused look on my face. I tried to laugh it off. "Haha, nice story, now let it go. Tell me, what is it that you want when I become the President?"

"You won't be the President."

"Now stop kidding. You know I don't like these stupid jokes."

Hari got up. His face was stoic, devoid of any emotion whatsoever.

"This is not a joke. I want you to step out of the Presidential election, and I want you to declare me our party's candidate. This is not something which I have just thought of, this is something which I have been living with for the last few months. It is only today that I have found a way to implement it."

He said this and took out a sheet of paper. The sheet had the photograph, of me and Radha- the Radha I had led to being murdered, my Radha. It was the photo which had led to the downfall of Surya and the victory of Prithvi in the Presidential elections when we were in the first year, it was the photo which

Privthvi had branded to end Surya's chances, it was the photo that had led to my political ascendance, it was the photo which had changed the picture of our University politics three years ago.

But this time, the photo also had my face on it. Clearly and distinctly visible.

But was it was the photo which was going to do exactly the same thing three years later?

I got up, my face red with fury and anger.

"You will never."

"What did you think, that Hari was always happy and satisfied playing the second fiddle. That you can make Hari do anything you want and he will wag his tail like a dog and listen. That poor old Hari should be left to his books and will ultimately one day make a civil servant. You mother fucker, I don't want to be a civil servant, I want to be the civil master. I want to be the minister."

I tried to regain my composure and think logically, but logic had failed me here. My best friend had failed me.

"Hari, you know how much I want this. And you know what all I have done for this. You cannot do this to me."

Tears were now trickling down Hari's face as he spoke.

"What all *you* have done for this? It has always been about *you,* hasn't it? Have you ever stopped to think that what all you have done, I have also done? The murders, the fest, the ass licking, the ass kicking, weren't we together in all of that? But at the end of the first year who got into the council? You did. And what did I get, the position of your best friend. The same story repeated itself year after year. You were the king, and I was a mere slave. And then, this year, when you had all the power, did you even think of nominating my name for leave the President, but any other post? Did you, Gopal?"

"Hari, I never knew you wanted to get into mainstream politics. You were always the outsider..."

"And why was I the outsider? Because you made me the outsider. Did you ever think that for once, just once, let's give some credit to Hari. After all, he has also worked his ass off all these years with me. Did you, Gopal? Did you?"

Tears were now freely rolling down Hari's cheeks. My eyes also started getting wet, I did not know for what. Was it the guilt that I had been unable to understand my best friend all these years, or was it the fact that I might lose out on the Presidential post. Hari continued.

"Gopal, I know what all you have done for this President post, but you know what- I have done one bit more."

I could not control my anger anymore.

"How will these photos help your cause if I kill you right now Hari? And you know I am completely capable of doing it."

Hari smiled.

"I knew you would say that. It is very difficult to trust a *friend* like you. I have programmed a computer to email a copy of this to everyone in Gandhi Bhavan after 2 hours. And only I know which computer has been programmed and only I can stop it. If you kill me, this photo anyways goes out. And not only you lose, but as was the case with the Gandhi Bhavan, for the next many years, Ambedkar Bhavan will stand no chance

in the elections. And I know you very well, the line of Brutus-
Not that I loved Caeser less, but that I loved Rome more,
holds true for you as well. We both know that you love the
party more than you love even your own political career."

I got up, and our eyes met. I could still see the same Hari
behind those eyes. The same Hari who had been there every
time when I had needed him. Who had given blood to me
when I had met with an accident, who had taken blows for me
when it came down to elections, and most importantly, he was
the Hari who had supported me when I had cheated on my
Radha. The same Hari was now standing in front of me, and
looking at me with the same eyes. The eyes in which I had only
seen love for me.

Hari was now also crying uncontrollably. He came up to
me and tried to hug me.

"You know Gopal, I still love you."

I slapped him. And then he could see something in my eyes
which he had never seen below, tears. Tears rolled down my
eyes and then onto my cheeks. And this time, I let them. I did
not stop them.

"I had slapped you two times when I saw absolute absence
of guilt in your eyes after exposing Radha to Prithvi. I believe
you can now see the same in mine. You can slap me once more,
I owe you that."

"Why did you do this, Hari? Why? Why didn't you just
ask for it? Why didn't you just say that Gopal, let me be the
President. I would have stepped down any day for you."

"Gopal, I know you would have. But the position of the
President is not what someone receives as a gift. It is something

which has to be earned. And I wanted to show you the ignominy in which I have lived these past three years. And now you will live it in the most important year. You will live as the *best friend of the President*."

"Since when have you been planning this? Please don't tell me that all these years of friendship were for this very day. Please don't say that. I won't be able to take it."

"No. This is something which Radha made me realise. And before you start thinking, no she is not aware or a part of my plans. She had told this to me around half a year back, that you are not treating me as a friend, but as an aide. And since that day, I have been wanting to get back at you. That is when it had hit me that you would be the President of the college, and I would be relegated to what I have been for the last three years, Gopal's best friend. I could live with that. But I would not have been able to live with the title of the President's best friend."

I slapped him once more. And then we hugged, and we cried our hearts out. We both knew that this was the end of our friendship, and we both knew how much this meant to both of us.

But for him, being the President meant more.

It had meant more than being in love to me at one point in my life, and I could not blame Hari for doing what he was. He had learnt it from his best friend.

He had learnt it from me.

I called for an emergency meeting of the whole hostel. Everyone had to be informed of the change in the Presidential candidate now. I did not want at least my hostel people to be surprised when they saw a different name in the ballot the next day. Such last minute changes were not allowed by the election committee but I knew Hari would manage that.

Hari and I waited in my room for the next thirty minutes as students were gathered from all over town where they had gone for last minute propaganda. No words were spoken in those thirty minutes, as we both lived the last three years we had spent together. We both lived our friendship, from the day I had come back to support him in front of the Gandhi Bhavan seniors to today, when he had stabbed me on the back for the post. Tears kept on rolling down our cheeks, but I knew that he was not going to change his decision. Because even if he did, things would never be the same between us.

After around half an hour, all the students of our hostel had accumulated in the foyer. All of them had been called back and were told that there was a big announcement. There was a strong rumor which had started doing the rounds that Gandhi Bhavan, sensing a historical loss, had pulled out of the election and that I would stand uncontested. Students were ready to celebrate. They were carrying colors with them along with alcohol and sweets.

I took centre stage, and took the mike. I opened with lines, which my best friend Hari, had read out to me a year back. Lines which the great poet Sri Harivansh Rai Bachchan used to introduce himself.

> "*Mitti ka tan, masti ka man,*
> *Kshan bhar jeevan,*
> *Mera Parichay.'*

(A body of clay, a playful mind, a moment's life- that's my introduction)

Good evening friends. There is something very important which I have to tell you right now and as always, I expect your full support in this as well."

My eyes were watering on what I was going to say, but I could not let the hostel see me in this way. I could not let them see their leader broken.

The crowd was expecting a victory speech and were kind of taken aback by what they were hearing.

"My friends, since the first year, I have received the unconditional and unprecedented love of you all. And every moment, I have put in my level best to be worthy of your love. But unfortunately, you will have to forgive me now."

There was a murmur within the crowd. They were all getting very restless.

"For the past few months, I have not been keeping in good health. Yesterday, I had some tests done, and the results were delivered to me today, by my closest and best friend Hari."

I looked at Hari, our eyes met, and he looked down.

"He told me, that I will not be in good physical health in the coming months. In fact, I will barely be able to stand and will need to be operated upon. Don't worry, your love will not let me die, but, I will not be in a position to be your leader, I will not be in the position to be your President."

The murmurs within the crowd turned to chaos. Students started shouting, started screaming and I had to make them quiet.

"I am sorry to have let you down. But I will not bow out. Tomorrow, when you go to cast your vote, in place of my name, you will see the name of my best friend and my confidant, Hari. I hope and I believe that you will support and serve him the way you have supported me."

I looked towards Hari and said, " Hari, will you now please come up and address our people."

I again looked at the students and spoke.

"My last words to you will be something which I learned from Hari. Something which Brutus had said to the people of Rome and today I say to you- **Not that I loved Caeser less, but that I loved Rome more. Not that I loved the post of the President less, but that I loved Ambedkar Bhavan more.**"

And I moved out and went towards Hari and hugged him. In front of 500 people of the hostel, I myself had announced the death of my dream. I needed someone to hug me, someone to console me. I needed a friend, and he was the only one I ever had.

The crowd went berserk. They could not understand what had hit them. Their leader had suddenly stepped down and given the reigns to someone who was only known as his faithful friend.

Slowly the restlessness of the crowd turned to admiration of my great sacrifice- relinquishing the post of the President for the good of the hostel and the party and they started applauding. Some burst the crackers which they had brought with them anticipating victory. Hari had to wait a good five minutes before the applause ended and he could say something.

And Hari was always good with his history, and he couldn't have started his note better.

"Good evening friends. I quote our first Prime Minsiter, Jawahar Lal Nehru, when India achieved independence.

Long years ago we made a tryst with destiny, and now the time comes when we shall redeem our pledge, not wholly or in full measure, but very substantially. At the stroke of the midnight hour, when the world sleeps, India will awake to life and freedom. A moment comes, which comes but rarely in history, when we step out from the old to the new, when an age ends, and when the soul of a nation, long suppressed, finds utterance. It is fitting that at this solemn moment, we take the pledge of dedication to the service of India and her people and to the still larger cause of humanity.

Freedom and power bring responsibility. The responsibility rests upon this Assembly, a sovereign body representing the sovereign people of India. Before the birth of freedom, we have endured all the pains of labour and our hearts are heavy with the memory of this sorrow. Some of those pains continue even now. Nevertheless, the past is over and it is the future that beckons us now.

Friends, it is not that we are getting freedom now, it is not that we are getting a new leadership now, but the challenges and instances that have happened in the past, should not be forgotten by us. Prithvi, Rakesh, Ajay- the three Presidents who I have seen in my life as a student in this great University, all strived for the same thing- to make Ambedkar Bhavan as strong as we are today. And this did not come about in one day. When Prithvi had won elections, Ambedkar Bhavan had come into power after 5 years. Yes my friends, 5 years. The lines which I quoted from Nehru, would have made sense then, because at that time, we had a tryst with destiny. But over the next three years, we have made our own destiny.

I repeat these lines to you today to tell you that we should not be complacent and should not forget all the hard work which has been put in by our seniors, and by our beloved Gopal, in taking our party where it is today. And tomorrow, when we go to vote, remember the face of Gopal, remember what he wants you to do, remember, he wants you to vote for your new leader- Hari. His own Hari, your own Hari. Hari, who has been with him in every decision he has made, who has been with him in every low and high in his life, and his Hari, who will keep on going back to him for support and advice. So tomorrow, we have another tryst with destiny, our own destiny which we have written for the last 3 years, and will keep on writing, for years to come."

The speech was a masterpiece. The adulation he received was far more than what I got and at that very moment, I knew that the day he became the President, people would forget me. He had shown me, and other seniors in very good light, but at the same time, had also shown the confidence of leading the hostel into a new era.

The crowd slowly dispersed and it was again Hari and I, as it had been many times in the past. The only difference this time was that he was the Presidential candidate, and I was the best friend. We both sat around for around fifteen minutes, and then he left. But before he left, he came to me. He looked into my eyes. I think he wanted to say something. But he did not.

I sat at the same dais for the last time that night. The dais which I had made my own over the last few months, and I wondered what life would be without it. I wondered what would make me get up in the mornings. What reason did I have left anymore to even be in the University. My politics, and my Hari, both had been taken away from me on the same day.

I don't know when I slept, but I was awakened by the first rays of the sun.

It was the day of the elections.

The hustle bustle soon started in the hostel. People were gearing up for the big day when Ambedkar Bhavan would once again show its supremacy over the other hostels. With me leading the pack, a historical victory had been predicted. It was now time to see what would happen without me.

I got up from the dais, and went back to my room and slept for another couple of hours. I so wanted this to be a nightmare, that when I wake up, I see the smiling face of Hari, excited because his friend was going to live his dream today.

I woke up around 11 am. The elections had already started at 10 am. I went out and got hold of a junior and asked him what the scenario looked like. I asked him what effect did the changed candidature have on the elections. Did it make people turn up in higher or lower numbers?

He told me that the already 50% of the eligible people had voted which was a record in itself. Hari had played the sympathy game brilliantly. He really did have a mind above those shoulders. He had made me the victim and himself the hero. The junior asked me if I would go and vote, if my health permitted me to do so.

I just smiled, and went back into my room, and slipped back into the nightmare.

I was woken an hour later by a barrage of knocks on my door. I had ignored a couple of knocks earlier but this was more banging of the door than knocking. Unwittingly, I went and opened the door. And there he was, Hari, with my, sorry, with his party seniors standing on my door.

Ram Avtar, a third year student from our party spoke. "Gopal, we have had a historical day today. More than 65% people have already cast their vote. We have now come to take you to cast your vote. I bet on seeing you, everyone who has not come out yet, will also come."

And I could not say no, this was after all my party, these were my people. So I went with them, to the polling booth.

General Secretary, I voted for Vikram Varshney from my hostel.

Treasurer, I voted for Puneet Singh, from my hostel.

Cultural Secretary, I voted for Prashant Panwar, again from my hostel.

And for the last and most important post, I wrote my own name with pen on the ballot paper and submitted it.

The results were declared in the night. I was sitting in my room all alone, and I heard the news from one passer by.

Never in the history of our college had we seen such a one sided election. Hari won by the highest margin ever recorded, he received 82% of all the votes which had been cast. All the votes which had been meant for me.

Soon I could hear a band playing, and crackers lighting up the sky. I opened my drawer, and took a couple of sleeping pills. I could not put myself through this. This was the day which I had practically lived for the last three years, and this was the day which was now going to kill me. I lay on my bed, the tears flowing freely and me not doing anything to stop them, and gradually, the pills started to get the better of me. I thought of taking more pills and ending all this in one go. But I was not that weak, or maybe, I was not that strong.

I kept myself adrift of all that happened in hostel and college for the next few days. I got the first hand example of 'out of sight, out of mind.' The same people, who till a month ago, were willing to sacrifice their lives for me, refused to even acknowledge me when we passed. My health, which was portrayed as the reason for my stepping down, did not concern anyone and not even once did anyone inquire about how I felt or how I was doing.

Slowly, I slipped into oblivion and Hari grew from strength to strength. The person who I had trusted the most in my life, had stabbed me in my back, and I guess more than anything else, it was this fact which did not make me strike back.

RADHA'S STORY

Politics can throw surprises at you and how! No one, not even me, the closest to Hari, had ever imagined that one day he would be the President of the college! No one had imagined that a plague will hit Gopal and he will have to back out and nominate his most trusted friend- Hari, to the post of the President.

Or at least that is what the official version was. But no one is as close to Hari to know the real truth. And that includes me. No, he did not tell me what transpired that day between him and Gopal which led to Gopal relinquishing the post for Hari. And no, I do not believe the official version. No one really cares now but if you look at Gopal, you know the only thing that is troubling him is the ignominy in which he is living, and not any life threatening disease. It was all a game, plotted by Hari and I don't care if I don't know the details.

Hari's behaviour had changed quite a bit since the day I had told him that he was a nobody. Fine, I had my own vested interests in saying that and they were fulfilled, though not exactly in the manner in which I had envisioned.

My plan had been pretty simple. I would instigate Hari, Hari would then go to Gopal and ask for a greater role in mainstream politics. Gopal, being Hari's best friend, would agree and I would be the girlfriend of a member of the student council. Being the girlfriend of a member of the council was any day better for my political ambitions than being the girl friend of the *President's best friend.*

My closeness with Gopal was growing per the day but he did not see me as anything but a younger sister who was the girlfriend of his best friend. It's not that I did not love Hari. I loved him a lot in the initial days. He was after all more famous and more powerful than an average Joe in the college. Being with him gave me a sense of security, a sense of importance. Boys in my batch were scared of me, girls in my batch were jealous of me. It was a beautiful feeling and a kind of a dream which I was living until I realised that I wanted more. Until I realised that I was not just content on being the *best friend's girlfriend,* until I realised that Hari would have to be more important in the scheme of things if I were to have a more important position.

And hence the outburst. Well prepared, well rehearsed. Hitting him where he did not know he could be hurt, and hitting him the most.

The outburst did not have the desired outcome of Hari getting a post in the council but then, as I realised over the months, Hari getting a post was just a mean to the end of more political power to me, and that is something which was fulfilled when Hari went into a shell and Gopal started interacting with me directly.

Gopal treated me like his younger sister, and that was way better than being treated as Hari's girlfriend. He gave me a hand in organising the fest and that was the biggest thing that had ever happened to a girl in this University. I now had my goals set clear. I had to be the President of the University, and it did not matter whether I used Hari or Gopal to get there.

After my breakdown in front of Hari, I had seen a marked change in his behaviour. Suddenly, he did not talk about politics, he did not talk about Gopal. In fact, he used to stay locked in his room for the entire duration pretending to study for the civils. I knew he was lying when he did not even fill the form for the exams. I knew he was thinking of something but I stopped paying much head to him once I got closer to Gopal. I did not think Hari anyway had the power to do anything.

As the fourth year started for Hari and Gopal, it was now my turn to play the king of spades. I would dump Hari, I did not love him anymore anyways. More than an asset, he was now a liability with him being in the fourth year and having no post. I would dump Hari and would get together with Gopal. I knew he had a weakness for pretty girls, all men did. And I tried many times to get his attention but I guess he did love his friend Hari too much. He could never see through those subtle glances and intentional touches and red blushes. I then thought subtlety had no role in politics. I had to go all out for him, and I had decided to do it under the influence of alcohol in the post Presidential victory party. But destiny had something else planned. When I got to know that Hari had replaced Gopal as the candidate and had won, I silently thanked the Gods for not letting me break up with him before.

I was now the girlfriend of the President, and if I played the game properly, I would see myself as a member of the council in the third year itself. And that too, the first girl to do so.

But this politics is a bitch.

I could have pretty well lived the life as the *first lady* in the University. I could have enjoyed the pseudo power and respect which comes with it and could have graduated to bigger things in the coming years. A slow and steady ascend to the top, especially for a girl.

But then this heart is also a bitch. And so is the brain. But the heart is a bigger one. Technically speaking, one pumps blood and the other controls all damn things that you do. But when it comes to matters of power, or at least what you perceive to be power, you really don't know who is doing what. And there comes a moment in everyone's life when you really can't make out what to do. So you listen to the first thought that comes to your mind. I think the first voice is the brain speaking. And when it comes to the matters of power and politics, believe me, always trust the brain. But then, the heart speaks up. And then you listen to the heart. Because what the heart tells you is way more difficult to do, but seems to be worth it. It always seems worth it. And that is where it all goes wrong. Because you always have to listen to your brain. Always. The brain knows the best. The heart should stick to what it does the best, pump blood. But then, the heart is a bitch. It makes you take a complicated choice. But in life, if I have learned something, it is that keep the decisions simple. But the bitch the heart is, it will never let you do that. It will always complicate, always.

And my heart did not want love or a good guy, my heart

wanted power. Ultimate power. And it had thought of a devious way to get it.

A few months passed by since Hari had become the President. As was obvious, he handled everything pretty well and had become a darling of the more important people in the central party. The funds were flowing, the University was running smoothly, all the girls were on his side, thanks to me, and there was absolutely no threat of any other party or hostel giving us any competition whatsoever. The margin of victory for us had been so huge that the other hostel and party had been practically wiped out. I personally made it a point to be seen at all important gatherings with Hari, even forcing him to take me along when he visited the more important people at the centre. We were practically living as man and wife and if this was the cost of being important, I was more than willing to pay it.

And on the other hand, Gopal had slipped completely into oblivion. He was obviously not unwell, everyone knew that by now, but such are the games of politics that no one really cared now. The same Gopal, who could make anything happen in this college, without whose permission you could not even move in the college, was now just another ordinary fourth year hosteller whose existence did not matter to anyone.

And therein I saw the opportunity. I knew Gopal would do whatever it took to get back at Hari. The Hari who had been his pillar of strength and who had duped him when victory was so near.

Three months after the elections, I approached Gopal. I now had uninhibited access into the Ambedkar Bhavan. I walked up to his room and knocked. There was no answer. I knocked again, again no answer. I tried the door and it opened.

Gopal was lying on the floor. The room was a complete mess. I don't think even sunlight had entered the room over the past few months. There was a terrible stench in the room of marijuana. Gopal had immersed himself in the drug to get rid of all the pains which he faced and I guess an overdose of it had led to the current position which he occupied in the room. I walked over to his limp body and checked his pulse. It was still there.

I let him lay there on the ground and got working. I cleaned the room, arranged the bed, stacked up the books and opened a window to let the light in and the stench out. After around half an hour of work, the room looked fine. I then picked up a bottle of water and threw the contents on Gopal's face.

Gopal woke up with a startle. His eyes could not adjust to the light coming in and he closed them tight only to be splashed with more water. He got up on his back, rubbed his eyes and finally his eyes figured out a silhouette standing in front of him. He rubbed his eye some more and realised it was a girl, and then he realised it was me. He was startled and checked if he was properly clothed. He was.

He got up and sat on the bed. No words were exchanged between us for some time, he just kept looking at the floor. Maybe he was embarrassed that I saw him in this state, or maybe he was angry at me because I, according to him at least, loved Hari. After around ten minutes of silence, he finally spoke.

"Who cleaned this room?"

"I did *brother.*"

The stress on the word brother a little too obvious.

"Why?"

"Because no matter what you think of me, I have always thought of you as my elder brother."

He was still looking down. He managed a laugh.

"Has that bastard Hari sent you to see the misery I now live in? Tell him that yes, he has finished me, he has finished me completely. If I had any strength left in me I swear to God I would have killed myself. But that bastard has even taken that away from me."

He then started crying, like a baby. The mighty Gopal.

I sat down next to him on the bed and he put his head on my lap and continued crying. I tried to appease him.

"No brother, he has not sent me here. I have come on my own. You are my elder brother and you took care of me when I needed it. Now in your difficult time I am here with you."

Gopal was still crying and asking me only one thing. "Why did he do it, Radha? Why did he do it?"

This was a very different picture of Gopal from what I had ever seen or imagined. This was a man who had been completely broken. I was still not sure what had broken him- betrayal by a friend or losing the Presidential post.

I let him cry, and then the tears stopped. He sat up and asked me again.

"Why are you here, Radha?"

And I repeated myself, in a little more emotional manner this time.

"The relation between a brother and sister is way beyond any relationship this world has seen. When a sister ties a rakhi to a brother, he promises her that he will take care of her no matter what. And I still know that my brother, my brother Gopal will take care of me no matter what. Today is Raksha Bandhan brother. I have come here to tie you a rakhi."

His eyes watered again. I had chosen the perfect day for this meeting.

The Rakhi ritual was completed and I tied him one.

"Sister, what kind of a brother am I? I do not have anything even to give to you. Tell me, what do you want?"

"All I want are your blessings."

"You will always have them."

There was some silence and then the question came.

"How is Hari? Did he ever talk to you regarding what had happened that night?"

"No brother. He said that it was between the men and I

should not interfere. And I did not. One thing which both of you did not realise was that that day, no matter who came out victorious, I would lose. One was the love of my life and the other was my brother."

I was playing the emotional card beautifully.

"At least he respected our friendship that much. How is he? How is the University, how is the politics? Does he ever mention me?"

"He does not have time for anything now. He is involved in the University activities most of the time, and when not, he is hanging out with the bigger leaders of the party, or at least that is what he says."

I said this and a tear trickled down my cheek.

"What happened, sister? Is everything ok between you two?"

And now it was my turn to cry. And as a girl, I can cry way better than a man.

The crying started with a few tears down my cheek. It then changed to a steady flow and turned into a full-fledged sob. I howled and spoke.

"There is someone else in his life now brother. There is some other girl. Everybody knows about it. I had seen them together many number of times earlier as well but always gave him the benefit of the doubt. But last night...."

Gopal was now concerned.

"What happened last night?"

And I lied.

"Last night, when I walked into his room, I saw both of them together and they were......"

And I continued the howling.

"He used me brother, he used me."

Gopal hugged me and wiped my tears and I continued speaking.

"Brother, you asked me what I want for rakhi? I want something and you are the only one who can give it to me. That Hari is a traitor, a bloody cheat. He cheated on you and now he is cheating on me. He slept with me, used me and now he has left me. I want you to......""

And I left it open ended.

But he completed it. "I will kill him for you Radha. I will kill him for you."

After some more crying and tears, I left. I had planted the idea in his head. It was now his turn to come back to me.

The plan which I had thought of was very simple. I would have to instigate Gopal to kill Hari. Hari had never told me what had transpired between him and Gopal that night. I asked him that whatever done and said, what if Gopal kills you?

And Hari told me that Gopal would never do that, because he loved the party too much to kill its President. He would never dare do that. His love for his party and hostel was much above his love for his own political ambitions.

And that is what had kept me in a fix over the last few months. I knew that along with the instigation about what Hari had done to him, if I could add a little more to it, Gopal would take the bait and not care about the party. I think Hari had judged Gopal incorrectly for once. I think he loved himself more than he loved the party.

And the relation which he had developed with me as a sister was the bait.

I had planted the idea in his head. I knew he would come back. All I had to do was wait.

The wait wasn't that long. He met me after a couple of days and told me that he was ready, he was read to kill. He asked me how would he do it and I invited him to my room later in the night.

I was alone in my room, reading a book, when I heard a slight knock. I opened the door and there he was, Gopal. He might be a nobody but he still had enough clout to enter the girl's hostel.

I let him in. He went and sat on my bed, his head at all times looking at the floor and not managing to look me in the eye. He asked me, "Is Hari still cheating on you?"

He now looked towards me and it was my turn to look at the floor.

"Where and when can I kill him?"

That was it. He was using Hari's (non existent) cheating on me as a grouse to kill him. But deep down, we both knew the real reason.

"Six days later is Independence Day. Hari has managed to get the Chief Minister of the state to hoist the flag. Hari will also be there on the dais."

"Why the Independence Day? Won't there be heightened security that day?"

"There will be. But there will also be huge coverage. Who will care otherwise if a student leader is killed? Nobody. But if he is killed when the Chief Minister is also there, that will make national news. It will give more sympathy to our party. Something good will come out of his death."

I was now speaking Gopal's language and he was understanding. I continued.

" You don't worry about security. All the security guys will be having a gun. And none of them would be that alert. This University is after all like their home only. We will manage to slip in our gun with theirs. Do you have a gun?"

"Of course I do. But no one except Hari knows about it. And he will be dead. But security will catch me."

"No one will notice where the sound comes from in all the noise. You can hide in one of the buildings and shoot Hari from there."

"But the flag hoisting for Independence Day is done in the football field. There is no building in the vicinity, and I do not have such an aim to shoot from such a distance."

I smiled. "I am in charge of organising the Independence Day function this time. I have shifted the venue. Now it is in the middle of the University. The science block is 50 metres from there. As soon as you shoot, there will be complete chaos and I will tell security that the gun was fired from some other direction. You can leave the gun there, and come down and mingle with the crowd. I will also act as your backup. Police will eventually get to you as you have a motive. But I will tell them that you were with me all the time. And they will have no option but to believe the girlfriend of a dead Hari."

Gopal smiled. For the first time in many days I would assume. I do not know if he could see through this plan. That I wanted to kill Hari more than he did. But I took my chances. I had to.

Gopal, "So it is done, six days from now, Hari will be dead."

Radha, "And what after that?"

Gopal, "After that, the University will get its rightful President."

He was right in that last sentence.

Gopal and I went for the final recce a couple of days before the flag hoisting and selected the position where Gopal would hide and shoot from. It was perfect, and gave a good view of where the dais would be. I had told him to be extra careful with his shot and not get the CM because if that happened, things would go completely out of control. Gopal smiled. The confidence in his smile was back.

Our plan was to put the entire blame on the other party at the centre, that they tried to shoot the CM but got Hari instead.

We had thought that we would hide the gun in the building a day before but changed the plan when we got to know that the police would take over the University campus a day before the event. They would use sniffer dogs, detectors, and all other modern equipment to check for any hidden guns or bombs. It may be a low security threat event but after all, the CM of the state was visiting.

And then the day arrived, the day the plan to shoot Hari was to be implemented.

15th August, Independence Day

The University was lively with students and faculty on the morning of 15th August. It was the first time the CM was coming himself to hoist the flag and it was a huge occasion for everyone concerned. I was in complete charge of the organisation.

The entire crowd settled in by 10 am and the car of the CM arrived with two other cars with security personnel. The CM was an ex student of the University and got off the car and touched the feet of the Dean of the University. I was also there to present him with flowers. I did that, had a few photographs clicked and moved towards the security men.

A metal detector unit was installed a day before by the police to take care of unwarranted ammunition. I had told them that this was not required as it was a low threat area but they persisted, and I did not as I did not want any questions raise d later. Everyone who entered the ground had to pass through the metal detector.

The CM passed through the detector, then the principal, and then it was the turn of the security guards.

The metal detector beeped very loudly due to the gun as one security guard passed, and then again when the other passed, and then again.

And then I stopped them.

Me, "Why don't all of you put your guns in this bag here and we will pass this entire bag once through the metal detector. The long beeps will stop."

As there was no perceived security threat, the security personnel did exactly that. And in that bag was already kept the gun which Gopal had to use.

The bag, including Gopal's gun, passed through the metal detectot and the guards took their guns. I personally handed the last few to them so that no one would notice the extra one lying there. After all were gone, Gopal came and took out the last gun and made his way to the spot which had been decided.

The event started. There was a small march past by our college band followed by host of performances. Everything was going according to plan. The dean of the University then came on stage to say a few words.

He was done in about 5 minutes. Now Hari got up and it was his turn to introduce the CM and initiate the flag hoisting.

Hari reached the dais amongst a loud roar of applause. Little did he know that this was going to be his last.

"Jai Hind my friends. Today is a very proud day for all of us. The Chief Minister has been gracious enough to take time off his busy schedule and himself is here to hoist the flag in our University."

There was a long applause.

"Sir has to go back to the capital of our state to do the same there, so without wasting much time, I would like to..."

And those were the last words he said. Before he could start with his boring history stories, a bullet pierced his forehead and he fell flat on the ground. A perfect shot.

As was expected, there was complete chaos as the bullet was fired. The security covered the CM and took him backstage and in the meanwhile Gopal had come down from the building and had joined the crowd which was running everywhere. But little did he know what was waiting for him.

Being the chief organiser of the event, I had the whole event video taped, and had placed a special camera where I had told Gopal to hide. As soon as the shot was fired I rushed into the security room and by the time I had reached, everybody already knew that Gopal had shot at and killed Hari.

I sat down on a chair there amongst all the chaos. The plan had been implemented perfectly by me. Hari was dead, shot. And Gopal would be caught by the police. Both of them were now out of my life, out of the life of the politics of our University. After some time I moved out of the security room. I asked what had happened and somebody told me that the police was running after Gopal to catch him and were in the market. I made my way there and when I reached, I could see Gopal being carried away by the police.

Our eyes met, I knew he had many questions to ask, but I was not in the mood to give any answers.

The next few months were to be played very smartly by me. I became the girlfriend of the dead leader who was slain by his contemporary, and I gained all the sympathy I could.

I would go an attend meetings, with important people, and would break down in the middle, I got the whole girl gang behind me and when the time came to nominate the new President of the University, I was the only choice.

The first lady, the first person from second year, to ever become the President.

And I had earned it.

EPILOGUE

I, Gopal, was runnin g frantically and I could see a sea of police behind me.

My short hair, all gelled, in stark comparison to the way they were when I had been running with Hari on the same lanes three years ago. I was dressed in a kurta-pyjama, Radha had told me that it would help me go unnoticed in the crowd. My attention then shifted towards Radha. Was she fine or had she also been caught by the police?

I suddenly did not know why I was running, and suddenly unsure if someone was even following me, but I was running. I looked back and they were there. I was leading them by a good distance, but I knew it was just a matter of time, just a matter of time before they got to me, the way the Gandhi Bhavan seniors had got to Hari and me three years ago.

Just then a stone was thrown at me which just passed my head. I did not look back. I kept on running. I could not make the same mistake my dear friend Hari had made. I got into the market, running over stalls, jumping around some people and crashing into some others. The market was as crowded as you would expect in a small town in Rajasthan with the narrowest of by lanes and a chief minister in town to hoist the Independence day flag in our University. A scooter was in front of me- it was a déjà vu moment. I had lived the moment before, but with someone else.

I knew what to do. I ran towards the scooter, and I pulled the man down. The plan was not as effective with only one person instead of two but the man fell down nevertheless. The scooter now occupied the by lane in entirety and the little man was under it. It helped me get a little ahead of the pack that was following me.

I ran more. I ran faster.

Just when I thought I had lost them, one of the chasers, in a last ditch attempt, picked up another stone and threw it at me. This time I made the mistake of looking back. On an impulse, I moved to the right and caught a person on a cycle, both of us landing with a thud on the ground.

I knew it was over then. The police came and hit me on my head with a gun and carried me towards the waiting jeep. The plan which we, Radha and I, had made was fool proof but somehow we had been caught. I wondered what had happened to Radha. Had she also been caught? If not, then I would not give her away. She was like my little sister.

Just then I saw her. She was looking at me from a distance. But still, over all that distance, I could make out what had happened. I was pushed into the jeep and was taken away.

10 YEARS LATER

I was with ten other men. Each headed in the same direction. All of them had a reason, or at least it seemed as if they had a reason. I just followed them.

We were in a cave, or maybe a dungeon. I did not remember much of it. And we were running. I did not know whether we were chasing or being chased. But we were running. Crawling, swimming, wading our way past whatever came through, but nevertheless, running.

And then there were the sun rays. I think I had seen the sun after months, or maybe it was minutes. But the rays hit my eyes hard and the sudden burst of light made my eyes go blind and took me back to a better world. A world where I loved, a world where I was loved, a world which had meant something, a world which had now ceased to exist, a world which I was not even sure had existed.

I woke up startled. I had seen the same dream all over again. There was this constant urge in the dream to run away from the jail, to finish some unfinished business. But I could never make out what.

I did not remember much of what had happened in prison

over the years. At times when I did get back my senses, I could hear other members of the jail taunting me that I was mad.

I was in one of my saner modes today and I went to the common area in the jail. I picked up the newspaper and read the headline.

"Radha Malik elected as the first lady MP"

Slowly it all came back to me.

The doubt on whether I should pull the trigger on my own friend. The sudden rush of emotions of all the years of friendship.

I knew all along that Radha was using me as a tool but I guess that on some level, my intent to kill Hari was more than hers. I did not know what she wanted out of his death, and honestly I did not care.

And then I fired the gun. And I killed him.

And as it emerged 10 years later, Radha walked out as the final victor.

THANK YOU!

Thank you to Jayanta Sir and the entire team at Srishti for their continued faith in me. This is my fourth book with them after 'Love, Life & A Beer Can!', 'If I Pretend I am Sorry!' and 'It wasn't love at first'. Look forward to your continued support in my future work.

Thank you to all my readers.

Thank you to all my friends.

Thank you to those who provided inputs to the story and for the grammatical corrections.

Thank you to my family.

Thank you.